Sentenced To Life

Jenni Fink

PEGASUS BOOKS

Pegasus Books
3338 San Marino Ave
San Jose, CA 95127
www.pegasusbooks.net

First Edition: June 2015

Published in North America by Pegasus Books. For information, please contact Pegasus Books c/o Christopher Moebs, 3338 San Marino Ave, San Jose, CA 95127.

This book is a work of fiction. Any resemblance to actual persons, living or dead, events, or locales is entirely coincidental.

Library of Congress Cataloguing-In-Publication Data
Jenni Fink
Sentenced To Life/Jenni Fink– 1ˢᵗ ed
p. cm.
Library of Congress Control Number: 2015942162
ISBN – 978-1-941859-28-5
1. FICTION / Coming of Age. 2. FAMILY & RELATIONSHIPS / Life Stages / General. 3. HUMOR / Topic / Relationships. 4. FAMILY & RELATIONSHIPS / Love & Romance. 5. BODY, MIND & SPIRIT / Inspiration & Personal Growth. 6. BUSINESS & ECONOMICS / Careers / Job Hunting.

10 9 8 7 6 5 4 3 2 1

Comments about *Sentenced To Life* and requests for additional copies, book club rates and author speaking appearances may be addressed to Jenni Fink or Pegasus Books c/o Christopher Moebs, 3338 San Marino Ave, San Jose, CA, 95127, or you can send your comments and requests via e-mail to cmoebs@pegasusbooks.net.

Cover Photography: Alessandro Alex Failla - afaillaart@gmail.com
Makeup: Tess Givnish - tgivnish@hotmail.com
Model: Kara Barling - KEB731@gmail.com

Also available as an eBook from Internet retailers and from Pegasus Books

Printed in the United States of America

To my friends, who everyday help me navigate the real world.

Thank you.

To my family who loved me enough to believe in me when I didn't believe in myself.

Thank you.

Finally, to all the companies who sent me emails saying, "While your skills & qualifications are impressive we don't think you're the right candidate for this position."

Thank you.

You were right.

"Don't feel guilty if you don't know what you want to do with your life. The most interesting people I know didn't know at 22 what they wanted to do with their lives. Some of the most interesting 40-year-olds I know still don't."

Mary Schmich,
Chicago Tribune '97

Sentenced To Life

Is a story of self-discovery, the harsh reality of life and the bright hope of dreams for the future. Chelsea Carlton spent the last four years away at college in California with dreams of becoming a hit fashion designer, catering to the urban working girl. Unfortunately after years of dedication and hard work she finds out the hard way that making it in the fashion industry isn't as easy as she thought it would be. Without even an entry level position to call her own she's plucked from the life she's dreamed of and brought back down to reality.

Her hometown is small, much smaller than she remembered and the tree lined streets she once loved feel more like a barricade keeping her trapped. New Jersey is no place for a budding designer - she needs to be in New York or back out in California but after letting her inbox get full with rejection emails it seems like she's stuck. She quickly finds out that the the problems she was able to escape start to resurface once she comes back home.

She hasn't heard from Chris, the guy who broke her heart, in almost a year but within days of moving home he's back in her life. The memories of their summer romance that she thought she left in California come flooding back into focus. Their trips to the beach, nights spent under the stars and his sudden and definite dismissal of their relationship. She should jump at the chance to be with him again but is the risk of opening up old wounds worth the price of love? After a run in with a long-lost friend the right choice becomes even less clear for Chelsea and with a looming party to celebrate her collegiate achievements she isn't left with a lot of time to decide.

Chelsea's life is full of uncertainty and suddenly she's forced to confront her past and make decisions that will forever change her future. Can she ever really forget about what happened and move forward with Chris or is their relationship best if it stays a faint memory? Should she continue to fight for her dreams or accept that life isn't going to be the way she imagined it? Staring down the crossroad of her life the biggest question she has to answer is, who am I?

SENTENCED
TO LIFE

As we drove, I watched the trees and houses blur together outside the passenger-side window, the humid summer air weighing me down, a constant reminder of my looming prison sentence. I'd spent the last five hours on the plane, thinking about the choices I made in the past, about what I should have done differently and how I let my life get to this point. I'd watched enough *E! True Hollywood Stories* to know that, most of the time, when someone's life gets derailed—they can pinpoint the moment when everything started to unravel. On the other hand, I had no idea when it all went so wrong.

"We're here."

My mom's voice shook me out of my daydream, forcing me to face the reality of the life that lay ahead of me. I stared at what would be my home for the indefinite future. My childhood home stared back at me.

"Yeah, I guess we are," I answered, my voice dismal and hushed.

Maybe if I say it quiet enough, it won't be real.

I grabbed my bag and got out of the car, my feet hitting the garage floor. It was official. I was back.

Merriam-Webster defines "perspective" as *a way of regarding situations, facts and judging their relative importance.* Throughout life we struggle to walk the fine line between living in the moment and gauging our emotions, based on the relative importance of an event on our lives.

Changing perspective means different things to everyone, but for unemployed college graduates, it means looking back on your life and wanting to start over—going back to those pimple-faced, hormonal high school days, and doing it all again.

Perspective hangs over us like an old romance, making us second-guess ourselves constantly. If I had changed one simple thing, maybe it would have made a difference.

Chapter 1

Welcome to the Real World

I opened my eyes, looking around, feeling the sun hit my face through the open window next to my bed—same four walls, same mix-matched furniture, same bedroom. I felt like an actor, going back to visit an old set—the scene was the same, but the part I used to play was long gone. Only one thing was different—me, but now none of the rest of the set seemed to fit.

I rolled over in bed and saw the time: 9:00 am on Monday. My first week back at home as an adult had begun. I didn't want to get up, but I knew eventually I would have to get out of bed and face the world.

I considered staying in bed until winter or until a job offer came in, but all that would have done was prolong my fate, and as bad as it was to face the world and unemployment, being alone with my thoughts was worse. I crawled my way to the bathroom in an attempt to save my last shred of dignity and assemble some sort of control over the free-fall life that I was in.

In college, it made sense for me to look my best every day, because between classes and socializing at the bars, I'd inevitably be forced to see at least a few people I knew, and I'd rather have failed a class than have a run-in with an old hook-up without any makeup on. Given my current situation, the only people I was going to see were my family, and they were required by genetic law to enjoy how I looked, makeup or no makeup

Throwing my thick brown hair in a bun, I threw on some makeup and forced myself to get dressed. All while trying to forget the fact that, I could stay in my pajamas all day and it wouldn't make a difference, considering I had no place to be today, tomorrow or any other day.

Dress Well, Test Well had been my mantra for more than four years, and until recently, it brought me enormous success in everything I'd tried. Despite my lack of ability at finding employment, I couldn't seem to give it up. Getting dressed every day was the one last hope I clung to that my situation would all turn around. If I had to feel the crushing weight of my life slipping by before my eyes, I at least wanted to look good doing it. There was no telling who I might meet waiting in line at Starbucks, after all—not that I could *afford* Starbucks on my $0 a day salary.

It may have taken me 30 minutes to figure out what I wanted to wear, but I walked out of my room with a new confidence that I'd recently lost. With a newfound positive outlook on life, I shut my bedroom door, leaving behind the evidence of my search-and-destroy method of picking out an outfit. On the floor lay the innocent victims of this morning's battle.

Making my way down the hardwood hall of the beautiful, five-bedroom home in the New Jersey suburbs where I lived, I smiled and thought: *I'm living the American Dream!* Unfortunately, by the time I made it down the stairs and into the kitchen, I remembered I was

22 years old, and due to a lack of being fit for any paying job, I was forced to move back into my parents' house. My American Dream came crashing down quicker than a tower of Jenga blocks. I was living the *Post-Graduate Nightmare.*

"Good morning, Chelsea! How'd you sleep? It must have been *good* being back in your own bed!"

My mom's genuine excitement for me to be home compared to my total contempt for this place made something inside me ache.

"Fine."

Just like that, my positive attitude was gone. I grabbed the box of cereal off the counter and started pouring myself a bowl. I'd always been a morning person, but waking up at home, knowing I wasn't on a college break, brought out the worst in me.

"Why are *you* up so early? It's not like you have to go to an office," I said to my older sister, Rachel, as she made her way into the kitchen.

Rachel is my big sister. She has thick, long blonde hair that dries in perfect waves and is one of those girls who looks better without makeup. People always tell me we look so much alike but besides the fact we shared the same last name, I never saw it.

Still, we were always being compared, and being two years younger, single and someone who blazed my own path—I was usually coming out on bottom. The centuries and centuries of sisterly competition, combined with how effortlessly beautiful she is made for the perfect storm of sibling rivalry.

With sisters, it's inevitable that one will always be the "golden child" and the other will be the "pity child," who spends family gatherings overhearing whispers from elderly aunts like, "Isn't it just the saddest thing how *she* ended up—especially when her *sister* has been so successful!" So, like most sisters, I *wanted* to see her succeed and be happy—only not as successful or happy as me.

I wasn't ugly, not by a lot if I was being honest with myself. I mean, we shared the same genes—so as her sister, second was still pretty good. My long brown hair had volume, which was nice, even though it never sat the way I wanted it to. Still, at 5'4" and perpetually two to five pounds overweight, I always wished I had gotten the cute, petite genes *she* had instead of the clunky, average ones *I'd* been blessed with.

Rachel was a two-year veteran of the post-graduate world, and was uninspiring to say the least. She was currently enrolled in the graduate school of life—busy getting her Master's Degree in economics, with a concentration on *the effects of a job market in a down economy*. She joined the family business right after she got her Bachelor's Degree, , the typical go-to for post-graduates who couldn't find work anywhere else. She didn't last long though. About a year ago, she'd started her own marketing company but because she had few to no clients, I wasn't really sure what she did all day. I'd probably end up in the same situation too if I wasn't careful

I'm not embarrassed about what my dad does or anything. He's the hardest working man I know and sometimes I even find myself getting teary eyed when I think about everything he's done for me. It just wasn't what I wanted for myself. My goals went far outside of this small town, and it was hard for me to see how working for him was going to get me there.

I'd spent the last few years out in California, working on perfecting my fashion design skills. My designs were innovative, exactly what the world needed but after reading yet another email saying, *you have excellent qualifications and an impressive résumé however we've decided to pursue more qualified candidates,* I realized that, despite a college degree and some pure, God-given talent, I was unqualified for the corporate world so I decided to pursue a more artistic route.

I loved everything about fashion; the way it told the world who you were, the ability to create something that effected someone's life daily. I guess in some way when I designed the perfect line for a young, just out of college girl it helped me cope with my own misfortune. The fact that I was vicariously living through paper dolls was sad if nothing else. Still, I just knew if I could get someone to notice me and design something that made someone feel good about themselves, it would all be worth it.

My sister and I had both been served a piping hot dish of life, and neither of us seemed to like the taste of it. I wanted to get out. I could feel it boiling inside me, but for the first time, there was no clear way to go. I'd felt the same way before, four years ago, but then I was able to apply to a college that was far away. Still, there was a sort of euphoria in not knowing —the possibility that I could be in a new place with new challenges next month, but that same euphoria was plagued by the notion that I could be in exactly the same place in six months.

Eyeing my sister from across the counter, I felt the resentment grow inside me, like a tumor that, left untreated, would eventually swallow me whole. Who was *she* to be lounging around the house? While I was stuck there at home, wasting away, as other people lived my dreams, she was *relishing* in it.

My frustration toward her wasn't anything new. We were close—closer than a lot of my friends and their siblings, but we were too different to ever really be friends. I cringed every time I felt my resentment rising toward the surface, and I hated myself for it, though "hate" might have been too strong a word.

I couldn't understand why I let her get to me or why I even cared what she was doing with her life. It had no effect on what I was doing with *my* life, and giving myself the award for *best at not having a job, but following my dreams* was like getting the award for Most Improved Player. It was a bullshit award—meant to lessen the ache of knowing you sucked.

Grabbing my coffee from the Keurig, I set out for my office, which I'd established over winter break a year earlier when I decided I needed somewhere other than my bed to work on my designs. I wanted to start my own line, which I found out (the hard way) happened to be every other designers dream.

Despite knowing how impossible it all was, I needed to try. Grabbing a tray table from the front hall closet, I set it up in front of the armchair in the kitchen, a prime spot for watching TV.

"Glad to see 'Mobile Office' is back up and running," my sister joked from behind the kitchen island.

I wanted to laugh, but I couldn't bring myself to give up my *the world is so unfair!* vibe yet.

The stagnant nature of my life left me with two choices and two choices only: joke about my situation, or cry about it. I made the decision early in life to save the *crying about anything going on in my life* for the privacy of my own bedroom. For the most part, I was able to laugh about my job situation, as long as I didn't think about it too long and no one else made a joke about it.

Mobile Office was the first result of this *laugh-now cry-later decision*, the "mobile component" being when I moved the tray table from the armchair to the couch. I thought Mobile Office would have become a real office by then, but with a serious lack of employers, it would have to do.

So I plopped myself down on the chair. Now was as good a time as any to start working on some new things. I'd made a few failed attempts at designing anything that was worth pitching to any stores but nothing had really jumped out at me enough to really pursue. Mostly, I got bored with what I was working on a few weeks after I started, or I decided it didn't represent what I was trying to say well enough.

Then again the need to design something seriously appealing had never been so real as now so I hoped my creative energy would manifest soon. I might not have been out there hitting the pavement forcing my résumé into the hands of every Fortune 500 CEO and possibly risking a restraining order but working on a clothing line no one would ever see was a step in the right direction, or at least a direction even if it wasn't the right one.

Moving my cursor to the little mail icon that served as the crystal ball to my future, I opened my inbox. That's when I saw it—a new email from URBN, the company that owned Urban Outfitters, Free People and Anthropologie, *and* was conveniently based out of my very backyard, in Philadelphia.

It was the *perfect* place to start my career! I could live at home and save up some money while still doing something that my parents could brag about at dinner parties. Plus, it was every young designer's dream to get hired there. I was about to get the job. I could practically feel it!

Subject title: *Thanks for your interest...*

It's amazing how fast life can change in your mind in the matter of ten short seconds. Maybe corporate business was the way I should go, after all! I imagined myself commuting into Philadelphia and spending the day at my iMac, working hard to prove myself—then heading to the bar for happy hour with my cool, new work friends. Maybe this post-grad thing wasn't so bad.

I was so busy picturing my new life that I hadn't even bothered to read the rest of the email. I didn't *care* when they needed me to start. I'd start right away if I had to, and I didn't *care* how much I was making. After working as an unpaid intern—*anything* was an improvement.

From: URBN CAREERS
To: Chelsea Carlton
Subject: Thanks for your interest...

Chelsea,

While your skills and experience are impressive, we are moving forward with other applicants whose backgrounds more closely match the needs of the role of Executive Assistant to Head Accessories Buyer. However, we would like to keep your resume on file, and should other suitable positions arise in the future, we will contact you.

Sincerely,
Talent Acquisition

Everything I had imagined moments earlier—my great new life—was over faster than it began. I tried to shake off the rejection, add it to the pile and move on, but not even the mindless numbing of reality TV could take my mind off that single phrase: *While your skills and experience are impressive, we are moving forward with other applicants...* It kept playing over and over in my mind, like a Carly Rae Jepson song, no matter how hard I tried to get it to stop.

What was even the point of *telling* me that? *My skills and experience were impressive, but you were moving forward with other candidates?* It would have saved us all a lot more time if they just wrote a big, "Fuck you! Enjoy collecting unemployment." in the e-mail.

I had internships, I'd been the assistant to a major designer—well, an assistant to the assistant of a major designer, and I'd even won national design competitions in college, but now I'm not even qualified for an *interview* to find out if I'm qualified to answer phone calls and pick up coffee? Those automated rejection emails were such bullshit! The only thing they meant is that *you're so unqualified you aren't even worth the two minutes it takes for someone to type out a rejection email,* and there was nothing more discouraging than having a pile of them fill my inbox.

I tried to convince myself that URBN was just one rejection and tried not to get upset. Sure, there would be other opportunities, but after being rejected for an *assistant* position, it was hard to imagine I'd find a job anywhere else.

Earlier in my job search, I realized I aimed too high, overestimating my worth in corporate America, so I lowered my expectations. Then I lowered them again, and again, and again—until I had reached the lowest point I could bear. While the job market had turned around since The Great Recession, it obviously hadn't improved enough. It had become harder than ever on the morale of today's youth.

A few years ago, no one was getting jobs because there were none to get, so adults felt sympathy for recent graduates, providing them with wise words of encouragement about how the economy will improve and life will turn around.

However, when the economy began to improve and some graduates began finding jobs in specific industries, adults began assuming *everyone* should be able to find a job—despite the statistics on the stalled unemployment rate.

So graduates who didn't have a job in "the improving economy" were left wondering what was wrong with *me*, why couldn't *I* get a job? All while participating in uncomfortable conversations with their parents' friends, filled with, "You'll find *something* one day!" and "Have you tried..." Yes, yes I have in fact tried that. Nada.

And if the insecurity I had about not living up to my potential wasn't bad enough, I had to see it in other peoples' faces too. Seeing yourself as a failure was awful, but having to face your missteps through the eyes of your parents, their friends and everyone who ever believed in you was excruciating.

Fueled by the frustration that comes with being lost in life and the caffeine from my coffee I opened a blank piece of paper and began drawing. That was it, no more self-loathing, no more wondering what I could have done differently, I was going to design the next hit fashion brand and when I was interviewed for my E! True Hollywood Story I would cite my Urban Outfitters' rejection email as the turning point in my life. By then they would be begging me to come work for them.

First it was a crop top, then a matching skirt and before I knew it I had design after design. I could feel I was really onto something, stopping only for caffeine I sketched for what seemed to be hours, days, months, who knows maybe my 23rd birthday had come and gone. I didn't care, I couldn't have stopped even if I wanted to.

My eyes diverted from the page for a half a second, just long enough to notice the clock on the top of the computer screen. *12:30 P.M.* I stared at it for a few minutes, assuming it had just momentarily frozen. In a minor panic I checked my cell phone for reassurance. *12:31 P.M.*

All of that passion, all of that blood, sweat and tears—*for only a half an hour worth of work?* I took a giant gulp from my mug and tried to recreate the same momentum I just had, to bring back that moment of clarity when I could see the pieces transform right in front of me.

"Oh, you're *home?*"

The voice of my younger sister, Sarah, filled the room, causing my thoughts to wash away, as if I'd never had them. I searched my mind to try to find that former fleeting moment of inspiration, but it was gone.

Sarah was a constant reminder of my better years—my high school years when I was 18 and had the whole world before me. More importantly, she reminded me of the days when I had *hope* about life. That was the funny thing about entering the real world: everything I thought I knew about life went out the window.

When I was in high school, I thought about how miserable I was and how I couldn't wait to get out of town and never look back. But sitting there at my Mobile Office in the kitchen at 22, I forgot the heartbreaks, mean girls and missed proms, remembering instead my high school years as "the good old days." Perspective is *everything* in life.

I stared at Sarah as she threw her backpack on the floor and flopped onto the couch, clutching her cellphone close to her face. She was about my height and her hair was always in perfect curls, a shade in between Rachel's blonde and my dark brown. We had a pretty strong bond. I guess you could say she's the bridge between Rachel and I, although she never took sides.

"Where *else* would I be?"

She had the perfect body, which probably resulted from many years of competitive soccer and a youthful metabolism. She would be going away to college in a few months, and if we shared any of the same DNA, she'd really thrive at school.

It was sad, but true. Graduation meant I had no reason for going to class, while being unemployed left me with no reason to leave the house. I couldn't afford to be somewhere else.

She laughed as she fixed an after-school snack. Staring at her, a wicked grin came across my face.

Go ahead and laugh—you'll be here one day too, and it won't be so funny then.

Then again, what if I was still here, too—four years later? Just the thought of being 25 and still at home terrified me.

"Do you like being home?"

"What do *you* think?"

"I don't know. I mean, it could be worse."

"Yeah? How?"

"Well, at least mom and dad are letting you live here."

"What are you *talking* about? Of course I can live here."

"I know. It's just some people don't have the same luxury."

"*Luxury?* You think having no job, no money and living at home is a *luxury?*"

"Better than having no job, no money and being homeless."

I rolled my eyes. She had no idea what it was like.

Chapter 2

The Past Comes Back

Ba-bing

That familiar chime, the one that went off at least twenty times a day, every day, the one that seemed so meaningless was about to mean so much more.

I reached over to the wooden end table, grabbing my phone from the glass tabletop. When I opened my text messages, I saw it staring at me, another ghost of better days gone by. While I couldn't remember my own social security number, I certainly recognized *those* ten digits—the familiar *215* area code was followed by seven numbers that I wouldn't have given a second thought to a year ago. It felt like my heart was going to beat out of my chest. How could something that once felt so normal feel so out of place?

Opening the text instantly brought me back to September and the nauseous feeling in my stomach when I read the "we're just friends" text. The only thing worse than being broken up with was being blindsided with a breakup. The kind of news that comes out of nowhere while you're making plans for the weekend and leaves you wondering how many memories were fake and how many things he said that were lies. Playing the broken-hearted woman was nothing compared to playing the fool.

Although I had appropriately completed all six steps of relationship grieving, seeing his number made it seem like I had never even entered the program.

> *Step 1: Delete every text he has ever sent you.*
> *Step 2: Delete his phone number.*
> *Step 3: After a few too many glasses of wine at your girls' night, frantically search social media to find his phone number again. Re-add it to your phone book.*
> *Step 4: Change his name to "Do not text."*
> *Step 5: Delete his number for good.*
> *Step 6: Forget about him and move on with life.*

Standing there, I found myself back at *Step - 1: Stare at your phone in amazement, while compiling a mental list of every reason he may be contacting you.*

The Renaissance had trusted advisors to help in times of crisis, in the 21st century, we have best friends, which is good, considering their advice is free as long as judgment isn't included as payroll.

Kenzie was tall, blonde and beautiful. Going to a bar with her committed most women to supporting cast status, as she was always the star, and if I was dating someone, I was always nervous he'd like her more. It wasn't her fault. There was something about blondes that made them more appealing than brunettes. Plus, she was carefree and knew how to play hard to get. I was uptight and available.

And the worst part? She was so used to getting attention that she didn't care whether or not she met a guy. She was content going out and just having a girls' night. She had been there for me through my worst times, including those with Chris, so after years of friendship therapy, she knew exactly what I needed. I knew I was able to confide in her without risking the chance of some bullshit "silver lining" confidence booster. It was not what I needed, not at that moment. She kept it straight, which made her the best and worst friend I could have.

> 12:35 pm: CHRIS JUST TEXTED ME WHAT DO I DO?!?

> Kenzie 12:37 pm: What did he say?

> 12:40 pm: Hey

> Kenzie 12:41 pm: Don't text him back. You're better off without him.

She was right. Of *course* she was right! After how he treated me, why would I even want to talk to him? I paced around the kitchen island five times before returning to my phone. What I needed to do was simple. I needed to delete the text and forget it. On the other hand, *what if he wanted to get back together?* Would that be such a bad thing? At least I'd be in a relationship and unemployed, instead of unemployed and headed for spinsterhood.

I wasn't half as miserable when we were together. In fact, I was happy—not the kind of happiness you feel when you find out it's 2 for 1 drinks at the bar. I was genuinely happy. I had a happiness most people never found. The only problem with mine was that I lost it. My phone was burning a hole through my heart. I grabbed it and typed three letters.

1:45 pm: Hey

Chris: 1:47 pm: What's up?

That's was it! It was done and there was no going back. I put my phone on silent mode, attempting to drown out the noise of the confusion in my heart. Without any socialization and a belief that all men were emotional sociopaths, I'd become a severe introvert when it came to communicating with the opposite sex. During the few times I had to, I panicked. Thankfully, I could divert my attention the *Sex and The City* marathon that was playing on *E!*

I lied on the couch in the kitchen, staring at the TV as Carrie's voice filled my ears. Her voice annoyed me, her outfits annoyed me and the entire *show* annoyed me! All she did was whine, when what did *she* even have to complain about? She had an apartment in New York City, a job she loved where she never had to go to an office, and apparently a money tree, planted somewhere in Central Park!

My bad attitude had reached a new level. It was one thing to get annoyed at everyone around me, but getting annoyed at fictional characters was a whole new low. I stayed on that couch for the next two hours, feeling sorry for myself.

My mom's voice was barely audible over my perpetual self-loathing.

"What do you want for dinner?"

"I don't care."

"You aren't going to spend all summer, lying on the couch, watching TV."

"Yeah? Well, find me someone who will give me a job, and I'll be sure to get off the couch. Until then, you can find me here."

"Something will come your way. You've got so many talents."

"I appreciate it, but your opinion doesn't really matter, considering you aren't in a position to hire me."

"You can spend a few days feeling bad for yourself, but you need to figure out how you're going to snap out of this, and quick."

I rolled my eyes. *Let the lectures begin..*

She didn't deserve my bad attitude. She had talked me through various mental breakdowns, had always supported me and had given me everything I ever needed. Something had changed within me that forced out my worst—a side I saved for only my most terrible ex-boyfriends. I didn't want to be so miserable to everyone, but I didn't know how to stop. I hated myself for doing it, which only added to my misery that caused it—a vicious cycle.

By 4:00 p.m., Carrie had left New York, gone to Paris with Aleksander Petrovsky and returned to New York with Big. I was so wrapped up in the fictional lives of Carrie, Miranda, Samantha and Charlotte that I forgot about my own problems.

There it sat on my phone—in the response waiting room for two hours. I was faced with a problem that plagued many a modern-day romance.

He didn't double text me. I shouldn't respond.

He texted me first, so he clearly wants something. I should respond.

He treated you so badly. He should suffer. I shouldn't respond.

If Carrie can forgive Big, you can forgive him. I should respond.

Was two hours too late to respond? What if he asked what I was doing? I couldn't tell him I was lying on the couch, crying inside. He would think I was still upset over him, which I wasn't. Obviously. Great, if I didn't respond, he would know I was ignoring him on purpose, and then it would seem like I cared, which I didn't. Obviously.

I wanted to give off the whole, *Oh, hello* casual conversation with the man who broke my heart and stuck it in a blender. *I'm completely fine without you I haven't thought about you once.* But how?

I decided to respond. I was an adult and it was the mature thing to do. Plus if I didn't respond then, I'd respond at some other time, probably after a few drinks, and who knew what I'd say then? But first I needed to close out of his Facebook page. It was hard to give off the vibe I didn't care if I was staring at his profile picture.

4:15 pm: not much, just been super busy.

Yeah, super busy—Netflix binge watching!

Chris 4:25 pm: yeah same, it's crazy.

What could he possibly be busy doing? Did he have a job? A girlfriend? Did he win the lottery?

Was he moving? I wanted to know more. It was like reading a mystery novel the moment right before discovering the identity of the murderer. It wasn't a choice at that point. I had to know. Unrequited love was a drug, and I was hooked.

I went to take a shower, which would buy me at least ten minutes of communication stalling, since technology hadn't advanced far enough to produce waterproof phones. Almost everything in my life had changed, except for my ability to do my best thinking in the shower.

As the hot water flowed over my head, I came to the realization that life had been much easier for my parents. What happened to the days when people had one phone, and they could be reached on it only when they were in their home? In the modern world, the reality is that people can be reached and reach anyone via cell phone at every second of every day.

Turn your phone off?—they'll find you on Facebook. Delete your Facebook—they'll find you on Instagram, and it went on and on that way for fifteen different social media platforms. Instant availability was great for the occasion on the highway when the gaslight is more of a demand than a suggestion, but immediate communication was detrimental to the mental health of all single twenty-somethings.

Interpreting text messages and mixed signals in the 21st century was harder than reading Egyptian Hieroglyphics. A simple text message, saying "hey," had an entire list of hidden meanings and secret intentions:

1. How's your day going?

2. Just checking to make sure you're alive
3. I love you
4. I'm bored
5. I'm texting you to avoid texting the person I really want to text so I don't look desperate.
6. Just have a quick question and felt bad asking you up front, so I've gone the small talk route

After careful consideration of the many different meanings of 21st century communication, I came up with my newest business venture, *Interpreting Text Messages for Dummies.* I could see it—a *NY Times* Best Seller, a nationwide book tour, fancy hotel rooms and maybe an interview with Oprah—it was going to be great.

Then, like most of my other get rich quick schemes, I found one fatal flaw with my idea—I had no *idea* how to interpret text messages. If I knew the first *thing* about interpreting text messages, I wouldn't have been taking an unnecessary shower, which would inevitably lead to spending an unnecessarily long time doing my hair afterwards, all just to avoid texting Chris back—which was all a waste, because the only place I was going that day was back downstairs.

Who was I kidding? I would have been better off writing *How to Avoid Awkward Encounters through Personal Hygiene for Dummies.* I'd been in the shower for 15 minutes, which was 10 minutes more than I'd planned on showering, so I turned the water off and grabbed my white terrycloth robe off the hook on the wall, facing the mirror and my reflection.

Mirror Mirorr on the wall, is Chris in it for the long haul?

I toweled off my hair and returned the towel to its rightful place—in a ball on the floor. I'd pick it up later...maybe. I pulled out my industrial strength hair dryer from the cabinet, and within five seconds, my hair went from wet and flattened to my head, to a full, blown lion's mane.

Another problem I didn't have before entering the real world —my hair never frizzed like this in California. I couldn't help but resent Kenzie, whose long blonde hair naturally dried better than the women in the Pantene commercials.

I'd watched my hairdresser blow my hair out at least 100 times when I was younger, but as an adult, it was time I did it on my own. How hard could it be? Taking a chunk of hair, I placed the brush underneath my hair and the blow dryer on top—forming a hair sandwich. Pulling the brush and hair dryer down simultaneously, I reached the bottom, twirling the brush back up the way I'd seen my hairdresser do so many times before. And then it happened.

I turned the hair dryer off, leaving it on the counter. When I released my grip on the brush, it didn't fall to the counter as I hoped. The brush had gotten so tangled in my hair that it dangled from the side of my head like a Christmas ornament. After tugging on it for a few seconds, I exhausted the last hope that I would leave that bathroom with a nice, salon blow out. I grabbed a comb.

Really? Is it so much to ask that one thing in my life should end better than the fate of the Titanic?

After ten minutes of tugging and hair ripping, I was free. I grabbed a hair tie and threw the rest of what remained of my mane into a bun on the top of my head. The messy bun worked for me in college, but since graduation, it was just another sign of the dismal turn of events that led me to living at home.

I went downstairs to the kitchen to find that my mobile office had been folded up and leaned against the wall. My mom was in the kitchen, starting dinner, and that meant one thing and one thing only: my dad had left the office and was on his way home.

For as long as I could remember, between 6:00 and 6:30 every night, the phone would ring, and my dad would say, "Can you let Mom know I've left the office and I'm on my way home?"

Before I graduated, I never really thought about this time of day much, but being back, I felt like a prisoner who received forced meals. I couldn't believe I'd have to sit there at the dinner table with nothing to say to anyone.

In college, I would have talked about any number of topics—something funny that happened during the day, the "A"s I had managed to secure, my plans for after graduation, and my plans for life for that matter.

That day marked the first time in 17 years that I had not one worthwhile thing to say. I thought about talking about the designs I'd gotten done, but even that seemed unworthy of the ears of people who were genetically bound to listen to me speak. My dad walked through the door right on schedule—at 7 pm—and we made our way to the dinner table.

Looking over the table arrangement, I realized how much our seats at the table said about our family dynamic. My younger sister sat at the head of the table—probably because that by the time my parents got around to raising her, they were just too tired to give her rules. So she ran the house, and she knew it. Plus, we were *four* people before she was born, so we sat two on each side. Instead of switching everyone around when she came along, they just plunked her at the end.

My dad and older sister sat on one side of the table, in a symbol of the bond a father had with the first born, the favorite. No matter what I did or how hard I tried, he would always consider the two of us by different standards.

We would never have the relationship I would have wanted, but I soon learned that, after I accepted what would never be, I was able to build a unique kind of relationship with him. Clinging to pipe dreams only pushes you farther from finding peace with reality.

Still, I didn't blame either of them, though. I blamed history. The firstborn has always been the heir, so a love for the firstborn had been deeply-seeded into our DNA.

My mom and I sat on the other side of the table, and when I wasn't being so horrible to her, we actually had a close bond. I knew both of my parents loved me unconditionally, but my dad had trouble understanding me—at least that's the way it seemed to me. Our personalities seemed so different. It was no wonder he couldn't figure out why I said and did what I said and did.

Mom understood me on a level that no one else did—she just got me. I think it's natural to gravitate to certain people within your family. Just because two people share the same DNA doesn't automatically mean they're meant to be extraordinarily close.

The conversation at the table consisted mostly of Rachel's work and Sarah's college preparations, but as the middle child, I had long since tuned out the chatter. Inherently, I was interested only in myself.

"So Chelsea, what'd *you* do today?"

Dad—I've been home for less than twenty-four hours! What do you think I did?

"Oh, I unpacked a little, and then I got some work done on a new line I'm creating."

I had unpacked my make-up but that was as far as the unpacking went for me, as boxes and suitcases still covered my bedroom floor. I wasn't ready to admit that I was going to call this place my home again, and as long as I didn't unpack, it was like I wasn't really going to stay. It was a nice place to live—spacious and well decorated—and my parents were easy enough to get along with. I just always thought I was destined for more.

"Really?" my mom asked. "You've been *working* on it for a few months now. Almost *done*?"

She could always sense when I needed attention, and I was always grateful for that. If I counted all my failed attempts, then yes—I *had* been working on it for some time.

"No. That was a different one. This I just started today, it's really cool though."

I left out the part that I only had a few pieces done, but the rest was true. So far it was cool. For once, perception was on my side.

"Don't most designers have a second job though? I mean, most people don't make a living as a designer until later in their life right?"

Rachel posed a valid question but with little other accomplishments on the horizon I was not pleased with being challenged. I used the only reference I could think of.

"Coco Chanel started when she was young."

"She's one in a million." Rachel reassured me.

"Wait, I knew you liked fashion, and I get you went to school for it, but no offense—are you even able to design a line by yourself? And who would buy it? Would you make it yourself?" Sarah inquired.

With that, my mom began clearing the dishes, signaling dinner was officially over. After decades of dealing with three hormonal, bickering girls, she found subtle ways of saying "Enough!" without ever actually saying a word.

Dinner may have been over, but I couldn't get what Sarah said off my mind: *No offense but...* Was that the new official pass for being rude to someone? *No offense, but you look like Free Willy in that dress*—as if not meaning to offend someone made up for offending them.

I guess Congress didn't know about the "no offense" escape clause, or there would have been way less protests across the country. *I don't*

*think you should be able to marry your partner,
but no offense.* I hated that phrase, like
everything else in life.

The exchange at dinner was enough
socializing for one day. With my newfound need
to shut my sisters up, I grabbed my sketchbook
off the counter and made my way upstairs to my
room. I'd never been much of a night owl, even
in the peak of my college career, but heading up
to bed at 8:30 pm was a new record for me.

Most people my age at least had the *I have to
get up early for work excuse*, but I didn't. The
truth was I could sleep until dinnertime the next
day without it mattering to anyone besides me—
and probably my mom, because she'd be worried
I slipped into a coma.

In all fairness, I hadn't been applying for jobs
for all that long—maybe six months at best, but I
still couldn't shake the feeling of gloom in it
seeming that my life didn't matter. Since the
dawn of time, 22-year-olds have developed a
strong desire to stand up for something, to make
their lasting mark on the world, have their voices
heard. It was all a part of finding who you were
and where you belonged in this big, wide world.
Our parents had Vietnam and Civil Rights, the
instinct was natural – almost necessary but while
most kids my age were discovering who they
were by moving to a new city and starting new
jobs, I'd lost myself somewhere along the way,
and I'd never felt more confused or anxious in
my life.

The purple carpet covering the floor of my
room had been installed in the 4th grade, at a
time when I thought having a Pottery Barn Teen

bedroom was the only thing I needed to have the perfect life. A decade later, all I needed to have the perfect life was a great boyfriend, a job doing something I loved and a nice rent-controlled apartment.

Until I was forced to move back, I never thought those were unrealistic expectations for life, but I'd learned none of them would come as easily as opening up a catalog. Growing up, we're taught to dream big – that we can be anything we want to be, we're practically force fed that shit. But there comes a point where you have to face reality and the reality is that you can't be anything – you can be anything within the box society says you're qualified to be. You realize life isn't going to look how you once imagined it. At 22 years old, my dreams—that once felt so realistic, seemed that they'd just be dreams, forever. Again, perspective is everything.

The walls of my room were originally purple, matching the motif of my 4th grade self. But that changed a few years back, after I watched *Across the Universe* a few too many times. I convinced myself I was a hippie and my mom and I painted my bedroom walls a light green.

I installed bamboo blinds on all the windows to go along with the green walls, which was one of the smartest decisions I'd ever made. The bamboo blinds were dark enough to prevent the sun from waking me up before I wanted, and they worked with my new dark and brooding self.

My bedroom consisted of mixed-matched furniture—some from the various stages of my life, and some that came as hand-me-downs from my sister. The furniture, green walls and purple carpet suddenly meant much more to me than just fuel for my memoir about how, as a middle-child, I was unfairly mistreated.

Life is about personal discovery, and the different parts of my room revealed that, at various stages in life when I thought I knew who I was—each time, I found out it wasn't really me. Looking around my room, I realized I may have felt far from where I imagined I would be at that point in my life, but I had felt the same way before, and things had worked out, so maybe there was still hope for me.

I flipped on the TV as I climbed into bed, more for background noise than entertainment. Thankfully, *Nick at Nite* had wised-up and traded *Full House* for *Friends*. Now I could fall asleep to the wanderlust of having a great apartment in New York City, instead of life lessons about standing up to bullies and being comfortable in your own skin. I was 22 years old, if I didn't know those things already, it was too late for me to learn.

I opened my Macbook—the one I intended to replace when I got my first paycheck—and I went straight to Facebook. Facebook was one of the greatest and worst things to happen to society since online shopping. On Facebook, it was possible to showcase all of the great things going on in life while simultaneously hiding the worst parts. Basically, Facebook's the Jewish mother you never knew you wanted. Sprawled across my newsfeed was the status I'd been waiting to see for months.

Hannah Morton: So unbearably happy to announce that I've accepted a job at Polaris! D.C.—I'm coming for ya!

Hannah had been my roommate during my junior and senior years of college, and we'd had a strange bond. We were pretty similar and had the same outlooks on life, and a few glasses of wine always led to philosophical conversations about where our lives were going. After a few tears, we usually concluded everything would work out, although deep down, I think we both were nervous it wouldn't.

Over our senior year, we spent hours making fun of the people who used Facebook to boast about their great new jobs or the graduate schools where they had been accepted. One night, I finally admitted I was jealous of them. I always knew things would work out for her—not because she was lucky, but because she worked hard and dreamed big.

It was warped that I could feel so secure in *her* future and that things would be all right for *her*, but when I examined my own life, I felt like I would never make it out of my parents' house. I guess it's normal to be your own worst critic.

The experiences of a post-graduate, trying to find his or her way in the world can be compared to a near-death experience: the result is enlightenment and a new perspective on the world. A few short months ago, we were laughing at Facebook status updates, and now Hannah was on her way. It turns out that people who boast about their lives aren't as annoying when you're on the other side of the fence. Again—the perspective thing.

I hit the "Like" button and closed my computer, deciding it was time to finish the sketches I started earlier and bring my designs to life.

Two hours later I was going over my earlier designs and adding some more shading to them. I hadn't gotten far but Rome wasn't built in a day. I messed with them for a while longer before stopping to really look at what I'd created.

The drawings were raw but for the last two hours I felt less alone, I felt less morose about the future, and more importantly, I felt like I had found something worth talking about at the dinner table. I closed my sketchbook; I didn't want to push my luck.

Laying my head against the pillow, I closed my eyes, feeling pleased with myself—until the sleep timer shut the TV off and I was left alone with my thoughts. All of a sudden, it hit me like a steam engine. *Everyone's lives were moving forward, and I was stagnant.*

I had my accomplishments during college: great grades, awards and positions in clubs. If I'd been an Olympic gymnast, the judges would have given me all 10s. But there I was, living at home, with no job prospects, and as much as I hated to admit it, lonely. Lonely was the one feeling no one ever was able to admit to feeling—depressed, happy, angry—all acceptable emotions, but not lonely.

I wasn't going to take full responsibility for my predicament. I wasn't to blame—not really anyways. It was the guidebook mentality that society had instilled in us since birth. Hikers use guidebooks to help them find their way through

Yellowstone National Park, and we use them to help guide us through life.

In high school, the guidebook told us to make memories with our friends, be active in clubs and sports and get good grades. The guidebook says, *if you do this, you will end up at the college or university that's right for you, and you'll be on your way.* Once students set foot on that university, they've officially opened the second guidebook.

Every year, 18-something kids leave home to discover themselves at college, forging their paths in the world. The college guidebook tells them to get good grades, find independence and grow into a young adult. The guidebook says if you do this you'll find yourself, four years later, standing in a cap and gown, walking across a stage with a diploma in your hand, finally you're ready for the third and final guidebook.

The guidebook to post-graduate life says, *you apply and secure a great job doing something you love, move out of your parents' house and eventually start a family of your own.* But what happens when your life doesn't follow that guidebook? College was supposed to be about personal growth and discovery, which is easier when a person knows the path they're supposed to take. The difficult part is finding your place in this world *after* college, when there's no longer a guidebook.

Half an hour earlier, I felt confident that something good was on the horizon, but lying there, I felt like a boat at sea where my navigation system was down. I was on my own.

Dwelling on that thought and with the fall of a single tear, I fell asleep.

Chapter 3

Housewives & Produce Guys

The sound of lawnmowers outside my window startled me from my dreams. Opening my eyes, I rolled over and reached for my iPhone, bringing it within inches of my face. With one eye open, I pressed the unlock button and checked the time: 9:00 am. I'd officially made it through twenty-four hours in the post-grad world.

Waking up at home during a break from college always made me feel secure and warm, but waking up and realizing I'd never be going back to school made me feel anxious—like I was going to cry and throw up all at the same time. I closed my eyes, hoping that when I opened them again, I'd be someplace different. To my disappointment, I was still in my old bedroom.

My life was consumed by uncertainty—no set schedule, no need to be anywhere or do anything, and certainly, no idea where I'd be in six months. Thanks to my natural body clock and my constant need to wake up at 9 am right on the dot, my type-A personality got a bit of relief.

Rolling out of bed, I walked over to my window and pushed it up. A rush of hot, humid air flooded past me, filling my room. To date, I had clocked 22 New Jersey summers, and every year, I was amazed at how thick air could be and how much it could weigh you down.

As I thought about the past four years that I spent in humidity-free California, any chance of a good morning went right out the window, along with the cool air from the air conditioning. Humidity left me feeling like I was stuck in slow motion where my entire body felt wet—it was awful! I hated New Jersey, I hated humidity, I hated everything!

I threw on a pair of jean shorts and a plain black t-shirt, making my way toward the kitchen. My internal tantrum about humidity had made me forget about the "romantic" life crisis that had occurred a short 18 hours earlier... until I heard my text message tone go off.

Chris: 9:45 am: Good Morning

How did guys know the exact moment when we stopped thinking about them? Was there an app for that? Since I had time on my hands I decided to search my kitchen, just in case there was some sort of hidden camera. While searching behind one of the four coffee makers in our kitchen, I heard a voice

"What are you doing with the coffee maker?"

Deep in my FBI-style investigation, I didn't hear my mom come into the kitchen.

"Uh, nothing." I muttered under my breath.

Turning, my mom went into the fridge, got a grapefruit and made her breakfast.

The go-to response for Generation Y had become "nothing." Maybe it was all the punk music we listened to in middle school, or maybe we just wanted to be mysterious. Whatever it was, it worked, every time. It's miraculous how versatile one word can be.

What'd you do at school today?
Nothing.
What's wrong?
Nothing.
What'd you eat for dinner last night?
Nothing.

For the most part, the response, "nothing," made about as much sense as Shakespeare, but parents accepted it so we kept using it.

"I have to run some errands today if you want to come with me."

That's what happens when you have nowhere to go and no one to see—running errands with your mom becomes a desired excursion. I began to feel like I was voluntarily checked into a mental institution, and my only way out of solitary confinement was to leave with a family member. I also knew that if I acted upset enough, we would go to Starbucks. It was a win-win situation.

It was undignified praying on my mother's compassion for her children, but I had reached a point where dignity was not high on my priority list. It would be good for me to get some time out of the house with the only person who would be sympathetic to my situation.

"Yeah, I'll come. Just let me know when."

I couldn't resist any longer, I grabbed my phone and typed out a response.

10:20 am: You too.

I didn't want to respond, but I couldn't just leave his message sitting there in my inbox. That would have been rude, and I was a classy, grown-up woman.

By 10:40, I was on my usual spot on the couch, watching bad TV, glancing at my phone every five minutes to see if he responded, which he hadn't. I knew I should have put something more conversational in my response. *You too* was such a conversation killer!

On the other hand, he could have responded with a question about what *I* was doing. One of us was going to have to light a spark in our conversation, and being that I was the one who cared more, I realized it would have to be me.

10:50 am: So big plans for today?

Double texting him was not my idea of playing it coy, I hated the way he had so much control over me—especially since I knew how the whole thing was going to end. Like I said, dignity wasn't really my thing lately. I couldn't help what my heart wanted, and my head wasn't strong enough to say no.

Chris: 10:55 am: Not really just drinking at my house.

Well, at least that cleared up the status on his job situation. I tried to form a halfway decent response to a 23-year-old man drinking at 11 am on a weekday, but I was too angry that he was still making me chase him, and part of me was still embarrassed and hurt from being so stupid about our "relationship."

An hour later, my mom was ready to leave. Walking to the door, I realized I had forgotten my cell phone, so I ran back to the couch to grab it. I was expecting important messages, after all. When I reached the car, I realized my sunglasses were in my room, and there was no way I was leaving the house without them. I had no idea how many gossiping housewives I'd see,or worse... ex-boyfriends. That was the problem with moving back to a small town—it was small, and there were only so many places people could go.

"Chelsea get in the car, what are you looking for now? This isn't a fashion show. We're just going to the *grocery* store."

"Mom! Do you want people to *recognize* me?"

"What does that even mean? You aren't Kim Kardashian. Get in the car."

Sliding into the front seat of my mom's SUV and buckling my seatbelt, I realized I had forgotten my chap stick inside. I guess I'd suffer through my chapped lips, because if I went back for it, there was a big chance that my mom would accidentally run me over, or worse—leave without me, and I'd be stuck inside again, all day.

I didn't blame her for being annoyed. People who were chronically late bothered me too. For the last hour, I'd been sitting on the couch, watching grown women argue about stupid shit. It was the type of show my mom considered to be "trash TV." Instead of using this time to get my things together, I chose to wait until it was time to leave. That was the problem with having nothing to do—it meant entering a weird state of shock when I finally had somewhere to go.

As we pulled into the Wegman's parking lot, I began to formulate my story. My life was a lot about formulating stories to seem more impressive. It was like being stuck on a perpetual online dating profile. I didn't like lying, but I just couldn't bring myself to tell the truth, which was too depressing.

It was my first time back to Wegman's since I'd been officially declared unemployed, and my heart began to race just thinking about being surrounded by all of the gossiping housewives who would be there. I felt like Daniel, in the lion's den.

"Linda! Chelsea! How *are* you? I haven't seen you in so *long!*"

She was headed our way, the ultimate nightmare of post-grads everywhere. My Mom had been friends with her for years and I'd been social with her daughter in certain situations, still her voice made the hairs on the back of my neck stand up. She was your typical WASPY housewife; attractive, overly interested in her children's lives and the biggest snob you could imagine. No matter how hard she tried to compliment you, it was always laced with an insult and you felt like a deflated balloon every time you left her. She was a vampire that remained youthful by feeding on the broken dreams of kids less successful than her own and I was about to be eaten alive.

"Hi, Mrs. Johnson. It's so good to see you, too! How's Jen?"

I had lived in the Jersey suburbs long enough to know how the entire conversation was going to work. I was going to smile and be polite, while she took digs at my biggest insecurities. One day, I was going to crack and say what was really on my mind, but it wouldn't be today.

"Oh, Jen is doing great! She's at medical school at Berkeley with her boyfriend. He's *wonderful*—he's studying to be a surgeon! Can you believe that? A surgeon! I can't imagine the work it must take, but he's so determined and been so *successful* so far."

My smile said *that's great!* but my mind was saying, *I'm disgusted with the pre-mature success of your daughter.* Seeking a self-confidence builder, I reasoned that, since neither of us were working and she was paying over $70,000 a year in tuition, I was still on top.

"So Chelsea, what are *you* up to?"

I looked around for a few seconds, her penetrating eyes were judging me. How was I supposed to follow up the newest medical couple?

"Me? Oh, I'm in the middle of working on my own fashion line."

"Wow that's great, is it difficult to get a new line in stores with such little experience?"

People constantly bringing up the fact that I didn't have a lot of experience was irritating but I had to admit it was true, I didn't have a lot of experience. Mostly because no one would give me the chance to have experience. Still, I didn't like it when she said it. I tried to discreetly roll my eyes.

"No, I mean, sometimes. It's all about who you know really."

"Yeah, I hear that all the time! So you know someone who works for a department store?"

"Well, no but..."

"Oh, a boutique store is also great for people your age!" What store is it?"

"Actually, I don't really know anyone there either."

"So who are you planning on working with?"

"Just, uh, connections I've made, uh, at school."

"Of course."

She smiled, she had won and she knew it.

"So are you seeing anyone special?"

Seeing anyone special? Where did that woman learn that it was socially acceptable to ask someone if they were *seeing someone*? It reminded me of people who thought it was okay to talk about their periods in public—or ever to *anyone*, besides their gynecologist!

I knew I couldn't lie my way out of the question. All lying would do was force me to explain to my mom how I wasn't seeing anyone, and then I'd have to sit through a lecture on *lying*, followed by another one on how I'd meet someone great eventually, because I was such a great girl. *Sure, Mom!*

"Not really."

I tried to force a smile, but I ended up looking more like The Joker.

"Well, I've gotta run, but don't worry—you'll find someone, because this has got to be the best you've *ever* looked!"

Was she fucking kidding me? Her words hung in my mind all through the produce aisle, though, *...this has got to be the best you've ever looked!* It not only made me irritated that she was still dishing out backhanded compliments, but it made me rethink how I've looked at every stage of my life. I wasn't overweight by any means, but let's just say there was still snow on the ground the last time I had gone to the gym. If it was the best I've ever looked, then I needed to get on my Facebook immediately and start deleting pictures.

"She's such a bitch. Still!"

"Oh, Chelsea don't let her get to you."

"But she does, Mom, because she's right! I don't know anyone who can help me."

"Have you even ever really sat down and thought about people you might know who could help you?"

"No."

"Okay, so it's not fair to say you don't know anyone."

"I just don't know why she has to constantly tear me down like that. It's just rude."

"I know, but it's just how she is, you know that."

"Yeah but it's been years. You'd think she'd get over it."

"Let it go, Chelsea."

I tried to think of something to say back to her, to make her understand my point and take my side, but there was nothing. She was right again. I resorted to silence and a scowl as we walked down the aisles.

If I was going to be stuck living back home, I was at least going to reap the benefits of a large food budget. I put all of the things in the grocery cart that I couldn't ever afford in college, like brand name cereals and milk that hasn't reached its expiration date, because I knew my mom was footing the bill. I'd never admit it to anyone out loud, but I began to feel glad I was living at home for a few aisles. I mean, it had its benefits.

Unfortunately the feeling wore off quickly. I found myself lost, deep in the analysis of the life of Chelsea Carlton, oblivious to the fact that I was about to run right into the guy restocking the carrots.

"Oh, sorry! I wasn't paying attention."

My face met his chest.

"Don't worry about it. I know carrots can be mesmerizing."

Was he flirting with me? I think the cute produce guy was just *flirting* with me! The mind is an amazing thing—in the ten seconds it took to exchange a few words, my mind had already began to picture our future together. All of a sudden, we were spending holidays together and shopping at Tiffany's for an engagement ring—all while Chris slowly died alone and miserable, preferably from some horrific STD, preferably one of those they had in medieval times that was particularly disgusting.

I shook myself from my daydream, awkwardly, realizing I'd been staring at him in silence for at least ten seconds, which felt more like three hours.

"Yeah, probably because you're so good on the eyes. I mean, carrots!—carrots are good on the eyes. I mean carrots are good *for* the eyes."

Well my first encounter with the opposite sex since I'd been back in town didn't go exactly as I had hoped, but at least it'd be a great story for the grandkids. I tried laughing it off and cracking a sensual half smile, but I ended up just looking like I'd suffered from a stroke.

"I've gotta say your knowledge on carrots is impressive. I should get back to work, but I'd love to hear your thoughts on *celery* sometime."

Was he asking for my phone number? Did he want to go on a date, or was he just being polite? Like I said, I suffered from paralyzing self-doubt when it came to the male sex, so I wasn't sure what to make of his witty banter.

I decided to just go for it, and if he was just being polite, I'd head straight for to the ice cream aisle, pick up a few pints and never return to Wegman's for the rest of my life.

"Yeah I've got some good celery theories too, here's my number, eight-five-six..."

He didn't even let me get through the full ten digits before interrupting me.

"Actually, take mine."

I'd had enough failed relationships to know that if a guy gave me his number instead of taking mine, it meant he wasn't that interested. I could feel my face getting hot, and I knew I needed to do something serious before I lost the last shred of dignity to the guy stocking carrots at Wegman's.

"Oh, I *see* what this is! You feel that you need to ask me out because you *think* I was flirting with you, and *you* don't want to feel like a *bad* guy. You're probably actually a pretty decent guy, but let's be honest—you're never going to actually *call* me, and I don't need to sit around *thinking* you're gonna call me, when you won't. Not that I *care* what you think—considering *you* work at Wegman's, but I don't *need* pity dates. For your information, I can get plenty *real* dates on my own, so enjoy your celery and your life!"

Well, that was that. I just verbally assaulted a kid who was working at Wegman's—probably to pay his way through medical school or something really noble, like taking care of his sick mother and eight younger siblings. I tried to save my dignity by defending my honor, though I was fairly certain I just lost any dignity I might have ever had.

"No, it's not *like* that! I'd *love* to go out sometime—I mean, a girl who knows her carrots is kind of my dream girl. I'm just not allowed to have my phone out at work, and as good as my memory is, I doubt I'd be able to *remember* your number."

The good news was he wanted my phone number, which meant I was still physically attractive to the male race and might not end up dying alone. The bad news was he probably thought that I wasn't only really mean, but I was also mentally unstable.

Hands shaking, I saved his phone number in my cell phone and walked toward the back of the store. Despite my minor mental breakdown, I felt so good about myself that I didn't realized my mom was coming toward me from the opposite direction. I couldn't decide if I should turn around and walk back the other way or just keep walking away from her until he left, while hoping she didn't yell my name across the store.

It was worse to be 22 years old and have my name yelled across the store by my mother, so I turned around and walked back past the cute grocery store boy. Armed with a witty one-liner, I strolled past the carrot department, feeling his eyes on me. I knew the only way to convince him I wasn't a stalker was to offer him an explanation.

"My mom—I thought she'd be at the *bread* section by now. Apparently, she's still in the *fruit* section!"

He cracked a half-smile and shook his head. That was it! I could not ever go back to Wegman's again.

Could this really get any worse?

It was about to get worse. I hadn't been standing next to my mom for more than thirty seconds when she pointed at him and said, in a voice that sounded like a whisper, but had the volume of a yell.

"That boy you were talking to was very cute!"

I was mortified.

"Mom, stop pointing."

"Oh, Chelsea—I'm *not* pointing. Besides, he didn't even *see* me."

"Yeah, but he isn't deaf, Mom. He can *hear* you. And you really need to learn how to whisper, because right now, you're just making a whisper noise and talking in your normal tone."

"Maybe that's a paid *position* somewhere, and you could get a *job*, teaching women to whisper, so they don't embarrass their adult-children."

I had to give her credit for being nearly as quick-witted as I was. Unfortunately, it was too soon to mock my job situation, so I rolled my eyes and bit the inside of my lip to keep a laugh from escaping. I thought for a moment that it was part of her secret plot to make me a spinster for life. That way, she would have someone to take care of her in her looming old age. Parents can be selfish at times.

Finishing up at Wegman's, we got in our car and made our way for Starbucks. After pulling into the parking lot, we walked toward the glass doors and green awning that meant we'd reached the Promised Land for caffeine addicts everywhere. Just as the hippies had marijuana, we had coffee. It was the signature drug of the 2000s.

The line was about fifteen people deep and curved around the basket of plastic mugs, but it was worth the wait. I reached the counter ten minutes later, right behind a thirty-something woman in a jogging suit, who stood between me and my iced chai tea latte. I listened to the mindless chatter between the woman and the barista.

You have got to be kidding me!

"What does the Peach Green Tea Lemonade *taste* like?" she asked the barista.

"A lot of customers really *love* that one. It's one of our newer drinks. If you like peach flavoring, you'll *really* like this one."

"Oh, I don't *like* peach. Hmm..."

Hearing this inane conversation, I scoured the menu for every drink containing the word "peach" in it. There was *one.* If you don't like peach, then why did you ask about the *one* drink that has the word, peach, in it?

My heart pounded faster as I grew more and more annoyed with the woman in front of me. People liked to think of Starbucks as some small, chic coffee shop, but in reality, Starbucks is just the McDonald's of the caffeine world. The menu was the same everywhere, so there was no reason for such non-committal ordering behavior.

The woman seemed to be better suited for getting her coffee from the Keurig in her kitchen than Starbucks. That way, she could take the time she needed to make this monumental decision without interfering with the lives of others.

"I'll have a black coffee with room for cream."

After all that angst over what drink, she had the audacity to order a black coffee! There truly was no justice in this world. Finally, it was my turn.

"Venti Iced Chai for Chelsea, please."

When surrounded by inexperienced Starbucks customers, I liked to display my level of Starbucks royalty by supplying my name before the barista even asked for it. I may not have been superior in the job market, but I was superior in the Starbucks world.

My mom ordered a short black coffee. As we waited for my name to be called, I got a new email on my phone. Was it possible it was a job offer? A voice inside was telling me that something good was about to happen—

something that was waiting for me inside the e-mail.

> From: Gilt
> Subject: Oscar De la Renta, Shultz, Vanessa Bruno, Stock Up Your Kitchen, Up to 70% Off. Start Today at 12 Noon.

And just like that, my feeling of great things on the horizon transformed into a feeling of depression. I'd grown accustomed to getting my hopes up, just to have them smashed, but I still couldn't shake the tinge of heartbreak when I opened an email that I thought contained a job offer, only to find it was an advertisement for something I could only afford if it were 100% off.

I glanced at the clock as I got in the car: 1:05 pm. It had been a half hour since the grocery boy at Wegman's gave me his number. Had I waited long enough to text him? In college, I would have waited until I was significantly intoxicated to text him, but seeing as how drinking at home with my parents only worsened my bad attitude about life, I couldn't wait to be drunk to contact him.

Since he was still working, I figured I should text him right away so that I would have at least a few hours before I needed to obsess over why he wasn't texting me back. Then again, what if he worked the morning shift, and got done at 1:15? Why did everything in life have to be plagued by so many questions?

I followed my gut feeling, hitting the unlock button on my phone I scrolled through my phonebook and found it—"Cute produce guy." I wasn't one for saving people in my phone under nicknames, as I usually went for the traditional first and last name approach, but since neither of us had introduced ourselves, it was the best I could do.

1:07 pm: Hey, it's Chelsea from Wegman's. How'd the rest of your carrot restocking go?

Going back to my inbox, I saw the same (215) area code that turned me into a rare type of crazy (that went just past Charlie Sheen level). His "Just drinking at my house" text was sitting there, reminding me how much things had changed since the summer and about how miserable I had become. Everything, even memories, were depressing in the real world. How did people ever survive this? Change usually brought me a newfound sense of excitement in life, but this time the changes in my life felt all wrong.

My fingers were anxious. I knew I was going to have to text someone, but since I wasn't ready to beg for an invite over to his house just yet, I texted Kenzie instead.

1:10 pm: Wine night tonight?

Wine nights had become a sort of phenomenon for twenty-somethings. Previous generations used wine nights as a way to share intellectual conversation about art or other sophisticated topics, while sharing a mutual love for great wines. In the 21st century post-grad world, it consisted of drinking as many bottles of $6 wine as you could, while discussing the men who wronged you, the jobs that you couldn't get and the things you couldn't afford. It might not have been the best way for dealing with our problems, but it was cheaper than therapy.

> Kenzie: 1:15 pm: Yeah! I get done work at five, and then I'll probably eat at home, but come over after! I'll text Ashley and Bridget too.

I had three great friends, and thankfully for me—they were all still in the area. I found people who had tons of "best friends" as untrustworthy—like they were making up for something that was missing in their lives. It also didn't help that these people usually made up nicknames for their friends—groups that sounded like rejected 90s girl bands. I hated when people did that.

"So Hannah got a job at that company she *interned* with this summer…"

The bond between my mom and me went deeper than just having someone to laugh at my jokes and build up my self-confidence when I was feeling low. Maybe it was the amount of time we'd spent together over the years, or maybe there were just some people you develop a deeper connection with than other people. Whatever it was, she knew that me bringing up friends who were getting job was indicative that I was feeling down on my own life.

"That's great! In D.C., right?"

"Yeah, she's moving there in like a week or two."

Mentally, I kicked myself for using the word "like" in an unnecessary way. Hannah wasn't moving to D.C. in like a week or two—she was moving there in *a* week or two. The word "like" was one of those annoying vices that no one noticed—until they *did*, and then they couldn't stop noticing it. I had recently began to take notice of how much *I* used it, and I vowed to stop as my post-grad resolution. Like landing your dream job, it was easier said than done.

"*You'll* get opportunities too, Chelsea. It'll all work out."

For as long as I could remember, my mom had always offered me the positivity I needed, just when I needed it. I'll never really know if she truly believed it would work out or if she had her doubts, sometimes it doesn't matter though – sometimes it was just having someone around who loved you enough to pretend.

"I know. It's just frustrating that everyone around me is getting job offers, and I have no leads or anything. I can't even get someone to give me an *interview*!"

"But are the jobs they're getting jobs you want?"

She had a point.

"I guess not. I mean, not most of them. But still, at least it's a job for them—which is more than I can say for myself."

"Stop comparing yourself to other people! The jobs they've gotten have *nothing* to do with you. It's like if you wanted to be an *actor*, and your friend got a job as a *singer*—the fact that someone hired a singer says nothing about the acting abilities of the other person..."

"Yeah, well—at least someone is giving *them* a chance!"

With that, I turned up the music.

Adele had been playing in the background the whole time—she was my *go-to* artist for the days when an upbeat country song just wasn't going to cut it. As much as I enjoyed my new favorite hobby—wallowing in self-pity, I couldn't help but think that mom had a point.

All through life, we compare ourselves to other people—how someone has such great blonde hair, while we have brown—the body of a girl who's 5'7", while we're barely breaking that 5' mark. That habit of comparison seemed insane to consider at all, let alone constantly. I compared myself to people who looked nothing like me, had jobs I'd never even considered applying for, or were dating people who didn't interest me. I made a pact with myself right then and there to try to *stop comparing and start pursuing.*

Ba-Bing!

> **Cute Wegman's Guy1:45 pm:** The carrots went well. Now the celery—they put up a fight. Thankfully, I was able to get them under control.

Reading the text, I laughed as a smile crept across my face. It was the kind of involuntary smile that came when something good was happening.

"Who is texting you and making you laugh?"

I forgot I was in the car with my mom and I couldn't believe I'd been so foolish to give her a glimpse into my personal life. I shot a sideways glance.

"Oh, it's just Kenzie. Something *funny* happened at work today."

I'm not sure why I lied. I had no reason to do so. I picked up the habit in high school where I lied for no reason at all. I didn't lie about everything—just my personal life, and usually, just to my parents. It wasn't that they cared what I did or took much interest in my life. I was 22, so what could they really do at this point? Well, they could have cut me off, force me to move out and make me pay my own cell phone bill, but besides that—what really could they do? I was honest with my parents about everything else in my life, but I couldn't bring myself to fully disclose even the most general detail when it came to my relationships for some reason.

I decided to seem less than available to keep an air of mystery. I wanted to wait a while before responding. I didn't want him to think the most exciting part of my day was going to the grocery store, after all—even though, at that point, it was.

As we arrived home, I realized I hadn't really done anything all day besides find my future husband, so I decided I'd sit down and apply for at least three jobs. By the time I got to my computer, I realized three jobs was a bit ambitious, so I set my goal at applying for one job. Lowering my ambitions and expectations was something I did more frequently than I wanted to admit. Reaching easy goals restored my confidence, and since I had no job, no job prospects, no boyfriend and no boyfriend prospects, I could always use the confidence boosters.

I hadn't always aimed so low. When I first started applying for jobs, six months earlier, I'd write and submit six or seven cover letters and resumes each day, and sometimes even more. As the days wore on and the rejection emails filled my inbox, I got tired of putting in all this work just to find out that there were 800 other people applying for the same job. The slow demise of the dreams of youth exhausts us in a way that many people very rarely recover from, it drains your physical and emotional strength leaving you in a puddle of lost faith in the floor.

Opening my favorite search engine, I used my crystal ball to determine what the future had in store for me. *Dear Google, what jobs are available in the greater Philadelphia area and require little to no previous work experience?*

Store Manager: Radioshack

Really? *That's* what my options were? Radioshack? I conducted a few more searches and finally settled on applying for what seemed to be a mildly interesting receptionist position at a small design house in Philadelphia. Double-checking that I had uploaded the best version I had of my resume, I clicked "apply" on the screen. By the time I turned on the TV to the E! channel, I'd missed the first two episodes of the marathon, but I'd still have about two hours left of *Sex and the City* binge watching. I put a pillow on the arm of the chair and rested my head as Carrie revealed her deepest insecurities.

Chapter 4

Four Girls & a Bottle of Wine

When I woke up to the smell of garlic cooking on the stove, I felt like I'd been asleep for days. My binge watching tended to turn into binge sleeping. It turned out that being angry at the world was an exhausting hobby.

I spotted my Mom at the stove, stirring something in a saucepan with a wooden spoon. I may not have had much intuition with men or career choices, but I had pasta clairvoyance and I knew garlic and a wooden spoon meant pasta. I decided to ask my mom to confirm my suspicions before I got my hopes up.

"What's for dinner?"

If the Carlton family was a musical, *What's for dinner?* would have been the main chorus.

"Ziti, with arugula, olives and cheese."

It was one of my favorite dishes, and given the recent attention Chris had been showing me over the past few days, I knew I'd probably have more than one glass of wine (or five), and pasta was a perfect dinner for that. I returned to the TV.

Twenty minutes into the usual dinner conversation about the success and interests of the rest of my family members, my dad turned the conversation to me.

"Chelsea, have you ever thought about applying for some more local designers? The competition is probably a lot less than New York."

"Yeah maybe you could design an item or two for someone locally. I'm sure they love to promote local talent!" my mom added.

"You could market it as a post-grad fashion line or something. I know my friends would be into buying clothes made by someone our age." Rachel was obviously feeling inspired by the idea.

Had I looked into local designers? I'd pitched the whole post-graduate affordable lifestyle line to just about every designer, boutique and cocktail napkin within 100 miles, no one thought it was worth investing in, besides my family I guess. I had to give them credit for their enthusiasm though, it was touching, really. I didn't have the heart to completely destroy their desire for me to succeed, guess I wasn't completely broken just yet

"Yeah I'll definitely look into it."

I thought my lack of a lengthy or enthusiastic response would end the conversation there but my family obviously had other ideas.

"You should really look into these recruiting agencies. I think you're making a mistake if you don't."

"Okay Mom I *will.* Can we not *talk* about this anymore?"

"Why are you getting so upset? We're just trying to help you," my dad answered, his voice accusatory.

"Because maybe I don't want to talk about how, after everything I've done, I'm not even qualified to get an interview *anywhere*? Not even as an assistant! Does that sound like something *anyone* on this planet would be interested in talking about? Can I be excused? I'm going to Kenzie's."

I didn't wait for anyone to respond. I just got up from the table and grabbed my bag and keys off the counter. It was the first time I'd ever stormed out on a family dinner, so I was worried that if I didn't get out soon enough, I'd not only be an unemployed 22-year-old, but I'd be an unemployed and *homeless* 22-year-old.

When I pulled up to Kenzie's house, I saw that Ashley's car was already there, which meant that Bridget was probably inside already too. By the time I got inside, wine glasses had already been filled, just waiting for my arrival. I also noticed a bag of red Doritos sitting on the wooden coffee table in front of the couch.

"Hey guys, what's with the Doritos?"

Wine had always been an intricate part of the wine night ritual and the more glasses of wine we had the more we needed to snack but Doritos had never started out as an appetizer for us, it seemed like we'd actually gone backwards on the maturity scale since graduating.

"Bridget said we needed to have a cheese and cracker plate because we aren't in college anymore, but I didn't have cheese or crackers, so I figured Doritos had cheese on them, so it was fine."

I was unaware of the new out-of-college wine night law.

"Since when is *that* a thing?" I said, shoving a Dorito into my mouth.

"*Everyone* knows it's a thing. It's *always* been a thing," Bridget snapped back.

As the youngest of six siblings Bridget was constantly trying to prove to us that she knew more than we did, the annoying thing was she usually did. She paid attention to things, things most people ignored, which proved annoying when you got into an argument with her but was also one of the things that made her such a good friend. She was able to know each one of us on a level that we couldn't have with anyone else, all because she paid attention.

Sitting on the couch, I grabbed my glass of wine and began passing my life problems onto my friends. What *else* are friends for?

"So, uh—I got asked out today at Wegman's, and Chris texted me twice."

And like that, all the air had been sucked from the room. My friends had been there through the entire breakup, so they shared in my fantasy of him getting hit by a bus. Even though we didn't even breakup, since apparently, we were never even dating.

Webster's Dictionary really needed to come up with a word for breakups that occurred when one person believes they're dating and the other person thinks it's just friendship. Maybe they could call it a "bend up," since they weren't really dating, and since bending isn't really breaking, it wouldn't be breaking up.

By then, I wondered if people got paid for making up words and getting them in the dictionary. I made a mental note to look up the payout for inventing new words.

Kenzie was the first to break the awkward silence.

"Wait, did he text you again after the *first* time you told me he texted you? You didn't respond, right? Wait—*did* you respond? He's such an asshole! Don't even respond!"

I thought about lying, my typical go-to for disclosing personal information, but calculating the amount of wine that was flowing, I realized the truth would eventually come out. It was better to just lay it all out on the table and accept my punishment.

"Yes, I responded, and we just had a casual conversation. Then today he texted 'Good Morning' to me. It honestly felt so good talking to him and just having a normal conversation. It was kind of like how it was before."

I hated myself for admitting it, because I *knew* how it sounded, but if I was going to go with the whole "honesty" thing, I wanted to do it right. I saw a mixture of sadness, hatred and hope on their faces. I understood how they felt, because I was feeling it too.

That's the great thing about really great, old friends—you share in each other's pain and sadness—not because society has told you to, but because, with certain friends you reach a point when you can't differentiate your friends' pain from your own.

"Don't *respond*!" Kenzie scolded. "He doesn't deserve it. Or at least if you're *going* to respond, tell him that he should just go *die* somewhere!"

Kenzie was the queen of giving out hypocritical advice. It was easy for her to tell me to forget about him and not respond, while she had been on again off again with the same guy for over four years. Come to think of it, we *all* had.

It was harsh and something I didn't want to hear, but what did I really expect them to say?—that they thought he missed me horribly and that he made a huge mistake? I didn't want to admit that I secretly hoped he would show up to the party Rachel insisted on throwing me.

"Why do we keep going back to these losers? I mean, think about it—we've *all* had boyfriends..." Ashley began.

"Mine *wasn't* a boyfriend... we apparently weren't even *dating*," I interrupted, mid-sip.

"Okay, Chelsea. But he basically *was*. Back to what I was saying, we've all had boyfriends, and they've all been great, but then they all turned out to be such assholes. And we *still* went back to them at least once. You'd think we'd learn something!"

"Hey! Matt wasn't bad, so yours doesn't even count Ashley."

"Matt acted like I was just one of the guys—who he just happened to be *sleeping* with! So yes, it does."

"Nope, definitely *doesn't*," Bridget insisted.

Matt had been Ashley's boyfriend for a little over a year. That was until she woke up one day and just didn't feel anything for him. I guess they just settled into a routine and the feelings got lost somewhere.

Isn't that how it always is though? You spend an entire relationship waiting for the day when you really feel comfortable with each other and by the time you reach that point you've forgotten what made you want to be with them in the first place. Still, she went back to him a few times but it'd ended for good a few months ago.

"Everyone fill up your glasses, because this is worth a toast."

As we raised our glasses, I wondered what Ashley had in mind. She'd always had a boyfriend, but for the first time in a long time, we were all single.

"Cheers to the men of our *past*! May they get run over by buses!"

With that, we clinked our glasses and gulped down a few sips of wine.

"Wait! Can we go back to the whole 'you got asked out at Wegman's thing?" Kenzie asked, transitioning to my new date.

It was about as subtle as when iTunes is on shuffle and the playlist goes from Coldplay to Flo Rida. Still, we all appreciated the change of topics.

"Wait! He doesn't *work* at Wegman's, does he? Cuz—no offense—but we always thought *Kenzie* would be the one to end up in a trailer park... but now maybe you will too."

Bridget was the type of friend who brought negativity to any positive situation. Oddly enough, it never bothered me. Part of our silent agreement was to hide our true emotions through comedic relief. It worked.

"Well, he actually *does* work there and we bonded over... WAIT! I forgot to text him *back*! I didn't want to seem desperate, so I waited, but then I fell asleep and forgot... Does six hours later mean 'uninterested?'"

"I mean, it's kinda weird," Kenzie advised. "Maybe you should just not respond now and wait for him to text you again."

"Okay, but what if he *doesn't*? I'm just going to respond, and hopefully he won't notice the time lapse."

I grabbed my phone as fast as I could, opened to his text message and sent the only excuse I could think of.

> 8:53 pm: Well that's a relief. Sounds like you had an exciting day at work.

By excuse I meant denial. I wanted it to seem as if nothing happened, because short of saying that I took a spontaneous trip to Antarctica, there was no logical reason why I would be away from my phone for six hours.

> Cute Wegman's Guy 8:55 pm: Yeah, well it was pretty exciting. See, I met this girl who was pretty cute, and after she accused me of being just about the worst person on Earth, she put my number in her phonebook.

I hated it when guys used the word "cute" to refer to anything other than a YouTube video of puppies. All I could think of when I read "cute" in a text was some weird, pervy uncle.

> Cute Wegman's Guy 9:01 pm: Sorry. That was weird. I never use the word "cute," because it sounds like something a creepy uncle would say.

I had never been so pleasantly surprised by a text in my life. Usually, when I was surprised by texts, it was because the guy I really liked explained to me, yet again, that we were in fact "not dating." A much better response.

> 9:03 pm: I'm not saying it was a deal breaker, but now that we've cleared that up, I guess I don't have to delete your number just yet.

Witty! That was good, keep up the good work.

> Cute Wegman's Guy 9:05 pm: Guess today's been a lucky day for me. I have to work early tomorrow, so I'm gonna go to bed but I'll be at Firebirds for Happy Hour tomorrow, and I hope you won't make me drink alone.

Happy Hour—the only remaining hope at a social life for unemployed post-grads. No one explained that when you finally turn 21 and can get *into* bars that you can't afford to *go* to bars. What kind of a twisted world is that?

"Ashley, did you hear back from any of the grad schools you applied to?"

"Uh, well I was rejected from three, and I'm still waiting on Villanova, but they said I might not find out until August 3rd, and classes start the 15th, so I'm not really sure how *that's* gonna work."

"What are you gonna do if you *don't* get in?" I asked, not meaning to make her nervous.

"I don't know. Work at McDonald's, probably."

"You can work at Applebees with me!" Kenzie suggested. "*They're* hiring!"

Kenzie had worked at Applebees during summers in between college, but unable to find a job, she reluctantly went back to working for tips and serving iced-teas to the mall rats.

"It's such *bullshit* that none of us can find jobs! I mean, we've all had experience and did well in college, but no one will give us a chance."

"I have to do *two* different clinical rotations, and my parents have a family friend who works at NYU. He said he was going to help me out, but I've emailed him four times and he's literally never responded." Bridget sighed, biting her nails.

"Yeah," Kenzie nodded, "and it *sucks* because it's like, once you've had a job for a few years, you totally forget that you ever didn't. Someone helped *them* get their first job, but they won't help *us*? I have a college degree and experience, and I'm waiting tables at a glorified fast food restaurant."

"Did you guys think it'd be this hard? I mean, no one really *tells* you it's gonna be this hard. They just act like you'll go to college, graduate and get a job," Ashley concluded.

With that comment, we decided it was time to change the subject.

Four glasses of wine later, amid an in-depth discussion about just about every problem the male race had ever bestowed on our lives—I suffered from an involuntary Tourette's fit.

"He is seriously just a terrible person! Like there are no redeeming qualities *to* him! He is honestly a horrible person!"

My eyes watered as I thought about how much I still *cared* about such a terrible person. I felt my heart breaking all over again. I didn't want to cry—it'd ruin the whole night—and I was tired of it all, but something inside me was empty, broken. I blinked back a tear as Bridget responded.

"I'd say *Mussolini* is the most horrible person, but Chris is definitely top three."

We laughed.

"Yeah, probably. It sucks, but they *all* do it. He's just a guy."

After finishing off two bottles of wine and a half a bag of Doritos, I decided it was time to head home. The best part about being stuck living at home was being within walking distance of Kenzie, which made wine nights less problematic, since I didn't need to drive.

"Bridget? Ready?"

I grabbed my purse and headed out the door, feeling the same hot, humid air that flooded my bedroom that morning. Bridget and I had been neighbors since the 4th grade and had shared countless summer night memories. She was a little shorter than me, with dark blonde hair. She was a comfortable friend, and though we had our fair share of fights—some of them brutal— friendship came easy for us.

We made it only one block before she gave in to the temptation and asked what we both were thinking.

"So what do you think you're gonna do about Chris?"

I took a deep breath before answering, staring down at my feet, as if *they* were going to give me the solutions I needed.

"I don't know. I mean, I still care about him, and part of me wants to be with him, but I was so broken after it ended. I don't know if I can really ever get over it."

"Yeah, that's understandable. Maybe you should see what he wants. Maybe he's changed. I mean, you *could* just keep things light."

Bridget was right. I needed to keep it light with him, but I didn't know if that was possible.

"I probably should, but I don't know if I can. How do you go from being so in love with someone to being so casual? I just don't understand how people *do* that."

"You think you *loved* him?"

"Yeah. I mean, I *think* so. It sure felt that way after it ended, but sometimes, when I think about it, I don't feel anything. I just feel numb, and if I actually *really* loved him, it seems like I would still have those feelings."

"Yeah, I don't know. Life *sucks*."

We had reached our houses, but neither of us felt like going inside, so we laid on Bridget's lawn, staring at the stars and soaking in the warm summer night air. I finally broke the silence.

"Do you ever miss high school?"

"Sometimes. I mean, not the shitty parts— like Brian dumping me at Prom or having to actually *go* to high school, but sometimes I think we were all just more fun back then. Why? Do you?"

"I don't know. I hated it when it was happening, but now I think I wish I could go back and do it over again."

We stayed there, lying in the grass while reflecting on the memories of our high school years—like we were viewing a photo album—

until the grass became too itchy and I had to head home.

After changing into my pajamas, I climbed into bed and, in my wine-induced haze, stared at the text from Chris. Maybe it was because I had too much wine, or maybe it was that enough time had passed and my broken heart was healing, but I gave in and texted him.

They say "time heals all wounds," and it was great that I didn't have to live my life with a perpetual broken heart, but in letting go of the pain of the experience, we sometimes forget the heart-wrenching lessons and become vulnerable again. Maybe it was better to cling to that pain, so you didn't let yourself make the same mistake with someone else. Again, perspective is everything.

11:25 pm: Why are you texting me?

I expected some response about how he just wanted to check in or his friends who were on his phone.

Chris 11:27 pm: I miss you.

I did not expect that response. I read it over and over and over again to make sure that I wasn't dreaming it, which I wasn't. I put the phone down, closed my eyes and tried to get some sleep. Twenty minutes later, I was still awake, and on impulse, I responded.

11:47 pm: That's too bad.

I wasn't sure if I wanted him to feel as hurt as I did, or if I was hoping he would give me 100 different reasons why he did what he did and why he needed me now. I don't know why I did it, I just did and he didn't respond—at least not before I fell asleep.

Chapter 5

The Harsh Reality

From the comfort of my bed, I could hear the raindrops hitting my window. I had studied abroad in Paris during the spring semester of my sophomore year and ever since, I had developed a fondness for rainy days. I forced myself out of bed and yanked on the brown cord, hanging from the blinds.

Grey filled the sky. I could hear the cars driving along the rain-glossed road. Standing there in my yellow floral pajamas, I watched the rain falling outside my window. I was overcome by nostalgia, which started deep within me and worked its way to the surface. I wasn't merely reflecting on the past—I could see myself there, back in Paris.

There I was, walking along the Tuileries, clear bubble umbrella shielding me from the misty rain. Memories of Paris overcame my emotions— and when I was there I felt in both my heart and mind that I was right where I needed to be, and right when I needed to be there.

In Paris, I discovered who I was and what I wanted in life, but somewhere in between Charles de Gaulle and JFK, I lost that sense of belonging. I knew who the Paris Chelsea was, but the person I was for most of my life, the American Chelsea, was nothing more than a stranger to me. I felt more insecure than ever before.

That's the funny thing about great experiences—they're simultaneously your greatest memories and your worst adversaries. Studying abroad was the best experience I had in all of my life—while it was happening, of course. Once it was over, it seemed my life would forever be downhill, a constant search for an experience that could resemble my time in Paris. It was like searching for Atlantis: time-consuming and full of disappointing dead-ends.

I pulled on a pair of ripped jeans, which I cuffed into capris, and a plain, dark grey t-shirt. Right before I was about to head out the door my phone rang – an unkown number on the screen.

"Hello?"

"Is this Chelsea Carlton?"

"Yes, this is her."

"Hi, my name is Alyssa and I'm calling from A.C. Bags. I'm looking at your portfolio and would love to talk to you about the assistant designer position you applied for, if you have a few minutes."

"The assistant designer position? Uh, yes. I mean of *course* I do."

I scrambled for my laptop as I stumbled over my words.

"First I'd like to talk about some of your inspirations and your time at Marc Jacobs. Your designs are quite impressive."

I was frantic as I searched through my documents for my resume and portfolio. I couldn't believe it was finally happening—someone who *actually* mattered liked my designs.

As her voice floated around me, I took a deep breath and began.

Twenty minutes later, I plopped down on the red arm chair that faced the TV.

"So Chelsea," my mom said, leaning over the counter to stare at me, "How was your morning?"

"I'm 22 and a waste of life. How do you think it was?"

"Nothing *unusual* happen?"

Her eyebrow arched and a Cheshire Cat smile crept across her face.

"No."

"Oh, I thought I heard maybe an interview?"

"Well you heard wrong."

"Really? Because it sounded like…"

"Mom, what are you doing? Do you have my room bugged or something?"

My voice was quick, irritated.

"No, I was just in the bathroom cleaning, and I heard one conversation."

"It was a waste of time."

"What'd they say?"

"We spent twenty minutes of her telling me how impressive my designs were, and then at the end, she was like 'oh, we're really looking for someone with more experience.'"

"That's great what she said about your designs!"

Her hands clapped together as her voice got more cheerful.

"That's nothing to just dismiss."

"It is when they still don't want to *hire* you."

"But Chelsea, you just have to…"

"Please, spare me the pep talk. I'm really not in the mood. I'm sorry, Mom, but honestly you don't understand how frustrating it is to be completely useless."

"Chelsea, you're not useless—you have so many talents."

"Yeah, and the one thing I'm really good at, no one thinks I'm good enough to get paid to do it."

"It may *seem* that way, but before you know it, it'll change."

"Mom, please just stop."

I could feel myself about to cry.

"I'll drop it, but I want to say something and I want you to listen. A year from now, I want you to look back on this moment and think about how far you've come."

"If I'm still unemployed and in this kitchen, don't bring up this conversation, Mom."

"You won't be."

She walked away and I turned to the TV.

I'd barely been able to scan the usual five or six channels when I saw the red, blinking light on my phone. As the wine-induced headache I woke up with faded, the night came flooding back to me like Niagara Falls, louder than any volume setting on the TV.

My heart was pounding as I felt that strange anxiety again. Glancing at the back porch through the window, I seriously considered throwing my phone outside and letting it sit in the rain for the next two weeks, but I knew if I was ever going to recover from my post-graduate depression, I had to start living. Facing life was the only chance any of us had at happiness. I just didn't know if I was ready to take that chance.

I took a deep breath, holding it for a few seconds, trying to still my heart. When I opened my text messages, there it was: Chris, in bold letters. He must have responded after I fell asleep.

Chris 1:15 am: Listen, Chelsea, I don't want...

Don't want what? It was all I could see in the text preview. I wanted to know what my odds were for a good result, so I made a mental list of all the things he could not want...

1) I don't want... *to hurt you.*
2) I don't want... *to be with you, just wanted to make sure you still know.*
3) I don't want... *to mess up your life, but I love you!*
4) I don't want... *you to be concerned, but I have a terminal disease.*

If I counted the first reason as a point toward "he wants to be with me," there was a 75% chance it would end positively. However, if I counted it as a point toward "he just wants to rebuild our friendship," then there was a 50/50 chance that his text would end in tears and more heartache. Why was I so scared to face the facts? I'd survived his rejection before, so I could do it again. I opened the text message.

Chris 1:15 am: Chelsea, I don't want to mess up your life or anything, but I'm down the shore, and I thought of you for some reason. I know I said some terrible things last summer, and I'm sorry I hurt you. I miss you.

My heart was racing. I thought I was going to cry, it wasn't happiness or sadness—it was as if every emotion I'd ever felt was fighting to come to the surface. He had written the exact words I'd been waiting to hear for months. Why wasn't I happy? It should have been the only emotion I was feeling.

Since August, I secretly wished it was him every time my phone beeped. I hoped he would be texting me to tell me how wrong he'd been, telling me that he felt everything I felt in July. I wanted him to tell me I wasn't crazy, that our summer romance was real.

I had imagined this moment at least 1,000 different times—even though in my fantasy, he showed up at my door unannounced and I forgave him for everything. I imagined him taking me in his arms and kissing me, and it would be raining, of course.

Talking to him used to feel so easy, but I tensed at the thought of it. Maybe there are just some heartbreaks that can't be mended, no matter how much time goes by.

I did what any rational, levelheaded human being would do: I deleted the text. *Out of sight, out of mind.* Who was I kidding? How could I face life and be on a path to happiness when I could barely handle basic human interaction?

I walked over to the Keurig and called Ashley. I wasn't in the mood for another lecture from Kenzie about how I should ignore him, and Bridget wasn't usually my go-to for serious conversations.

"Hey, what's up?"

"Chris texted me again."

"Yeah? What'd he say?"

"That he misses me, he's sorry. Pretty much what they all say."

"Wow, have you told Kenzie or Bridget yet?"

"No, I'm really not in the mood to be lectured on how I need to ignore him."

"Yeah, I get that. She's a little aggressive when it comes to that stuff, but it's only because she cares, you know?"

"I know, but sometimes I'm just not in the mood for it—especially from her."

"Why especially from her?" she asked laughing.

"Because of how hypocritical it is. She's been on again and off again with Joe more times than I can even count, but she thinks she's one to give me advice?"

"Okay, but you *know* how hard it's been for her. I don't think she's ever really gotten over it. It wasn't exactly a good breakup."

"Are they ever?"

"Good point. Anyways, did you respond to Chris?"

"No, not yet."

"Are you going to?"

"I don't know. Sometimes I want to, because it'd be so much easier, but then when I'm about to do it, I'm not even sure if I like him anymore."

"That's exactly how it was with Matt and me! When we were fighting, all I wanted was for us to not be fighting, but once we weren't fighting, I realized I didn't like him anymore. It was like anger was the only emotion I could feel towards him."

"Do you guys talk at all anymore?"

"Not really... the casual 'Merry Christmas' or 'Happy Birthday' text, but not much more."

"Wow, it's so weird to think about it being really over."

"I know, but we both just reached a point when we weren't interested in faking it just because we were scared to move on. So we just slowly stopped talking, and then enough time went by that the silence felt normal."

"That's crazy."

"I know. I've gotta go, though. My mom's yelling at me to empty the dishwasher, but let me know how it goes with Chris."

"Yeah, I will. Bye."

As we hung up, I had an epiphany. There's a saying that *you have to kiss a lot of frogs before you find your prince.* But what if, in the end, you find yourself back with one of those *frog*s? Did it mean that all the stuff in between the breakup and the present was a waste of time?

Maybe life isn't made up of a beginning, middle and end. Maybe life is actually as The Lion Circle suggests, a circle—maybe it is a matter of repeating the same mistakes and going around and around, revisiting old relationships until two people mutually realized each other were the best they were going to get. Maybe there aren't soul mates and people aren't destined to be with each other. Maybe love was one big consolation prize.

Thankfully, the familiar putt-putt end of the Keurig cycle diverted me from my depressing philosophical realization. I grabbed the blue ceramic mug from the machine and headed for the sunroom. It was still raining, so I decided to catch up on some long procrastinated reading.

Sprawling out on the yellow floral cushions that covered the wicker bench, I opened *Les Miserables* to page 947 and began to read. I had started the book in April of the previous year, hoping to finish the lengthy novel by the end of summer. Since I never specified *which* summer was my goal, I could achieve it by finishing in August. Couldn't Victor Hugo have learned the art of *less is more*?

Twenty minutes later, the barricades had been constructed, the revolution had begun and Marius had confessed his love to Cossette. I decided it was a good stopping point, so I closed the book and turned my head toward the window.

The sunroom was one of the few luxuries of living at home that I enjoyed. Three of its walls were windows, so as I sat there on rainy days, I was grateful I didn't have a job. Though it seemed I had been staring out at the rain for what seemed like hours, it had actually been 2½ minutes. Rachel startled me from the daydream.

"We need to figure out some stuff for the party on Friday."

Despite the fact that I had graduated without any major accomplishments to mention, and I was officially "unemployed," my family's decision to throw a party to celebrate my lack of achievement in the post grad world was still a go. In my romantic turmoil, I had completely forgotten about the party.

"Like *what*? We'll get the alcohol and cups on Friday afternoon sometime, and I *think* Mom and

Dad are taking care of the food. It's just going to be casual. I don't even know why we're *having* this stupid thing."

"Uh, maybe because you just graduated *college*? What's *wrong* with you?"

"There's nothing to really celebrate. Getting through college was pretty easy. It's not like I went to *Harvard* or anything."

"Okay, well we're having it. So who of your friends is coming?"

Good question. Sure, I had invited them all to the Facebook event page, but I hadn't actually talked to anyone about it. Plus, I wasn't too worried about anyone else, considering we were all broke and the alcohol would be free. I knew they would show. I assumed Kenzie, Bridget and Ashley would be there. Social media provided the illusion of being connected to people even though there had been no actual communication in weeks.

"I'll text everyone to remind them later today. Who of *Matt's* friends are coming?"

Matt was my sister's long term boyfriend, and coincidentally, Chris's *brother.* That infinitely small detail forced me to live in terror every time we had a party at our house or I chose to go to the bar with them. He was like the stomach flu—you never knew when he was going to show up. Only when he came around, I didn't lose five pounds.

My sisters and I were nothing like *Little Women*, despite all my mom's hopes that we would be, but we were close enough, so that when I asked the question, Rachel knew what I really meant.

Was Chris coming? Did he have a girlfriend? Was his girlfriend pretty? Did he still love me? Can you uninvite him?

One of my biggest fears was that Rachel and Matt would get married, and after having to go dateless to the wedding, I'd be relegated to spending major holidays with Chris and his inevitably gorgeous wife, while I remained single and living at home, with only my eight cats to keep me company.

Sure, it wasn't rational fear, considering Matt hadn't even proposed to Rachel and I still had years to find a husband, but I figured that if people could be scared of ketchup, then I could be scared of spending the holidays single—with the man who broke my heart.

"The usual suspects. I know he didn't specifically invite Chris, but who knows if he'll end up coming anyway," Rachel answered in such a casual manner that I questioned her sanity.

There is nothing insignificant about his presence at my party!

"I don't really understand why he'd come if he wasn't invited," I reasoned.

"Well, I didn't specifically invite any of Matt's friends, but they *are* brothers and they have the same friends, so I'm sure he's heard about it."

"Yeah, but *who* does what he did to me and then would have the nerve to show up at a party for me—at my *own* house? I mean, really—only a sociopath would do that!"

"I don't know what to tell you. Maybe he *is* a sociopath."

"Maybe."

I knew what would happen if he came, but part of me hoped he would show up. While I knew I'd end up following him around all night, begging for unrequited attention, adding to my heartache and disaster, I probably would put myself in that situation anyway. My disappointment with my employment status had left me feeling numb about everything in life, so part of me, on some demented level, enjoyed the pain of heartbreak. What can I say? I'm an emotional terrorist.

I could hear my sister yelling to me from the kitchen.

"I'm making pizza for lunch. Do you want some?"

No, I didn't want some! I wasn't hungry at all!

"Sure! I mean, if you put it in front of me, I'm going to eat it."

I never understood people who chose not to eat just because they weren't hungry. How did they resist the smell of pizza, fresh out of the oven? I felt very little shame in overeating and my lack of self-control.

I swapped the bench in the sunroom for the orange couch in the kitchen. I had stimulated my mind enough with reading, so I opened my laptop. The background to my computer was Holly Golightly's townhome from *Breakfast at Tiffany's*. I'd set it as my background, to serve as constant motivation. My goal was to get a great job, move to New York City and really become a success story.

I was pretty far from that goal but I couldn't seem to make myself change the background. Changing it would be the equivalent of admitting defeat, accepting that I had lost my battle to the real world.

When my phone vibrated from my pocket, I grabbed it, hoping it was one of my friends, asking if I wanted to drink, rather than Chris, taking back what he had just sent me.

I opened up my sketchbook and stared at what I'd done the day before. I wanted to find some fault with them, some reason as to why they weren't good enough, why I wasn't good enough, but I couldn't. They were good—even through my clouded judgment on life, I could tell they were good. I just didn't understand how if I thought they were good, and the people I showed them to thought they were good, how it was possible that no one who actually mattered could think they were good.

Rachel brought me a slice of pizza and I took a big bite. It was boiling hot, and as I tried to get some cool air into my mouth, a big chunk of mozzarella cheese and tomato sauce fell off the slice and landed on my sketchbook.

"Fuck! Are you *kidding* me?"

I frantically searched for a napkin to wipe it off.

"Calm down. I'll get a napkin."

"I just don't understand why everything has to go wrong in my life! Seriously, everything I go to do ends up terribly," I complained as I tried to save my sketches. *Blot, don't rub*, my Mom's echoed in my head

After a few minutes, I broke the silence.

"I have a date tonight."

I don't know if was experiencing a Tourette outburst or wanted her to know I wasn't a complete spinster yet.

"With who?"

Valid question. I was about to answer it when I realized I'd never even gotten the name of the cute guy who worked at Wegman's.

"This guy I met yesterday. He works at Wegman's. We're going to Firebirds for Happy Hour."

I found in life that the best way to avoid disclosing information is by over sharing other information.

"*That's* exciting!"

"I guess. It's not like I'd really ever date anyone from around here, though."

"Why not?"

"Uh, maybe because I don't want to *stay* here?"

"Yeah? Well, you never know."

Like most other positive things in life, I cringed at the thought. At that point, I hadn't brought anyone home as my actual boyfriend in over four years, so I thought my family had made the assumption that I'd be one of those overly successful businesswomen who sacrificed their relationships for their career. I'd thought that too, for a while—until I realized I had no boyfriend or career.

I'd never been one for relationships—partially because I enjoyed being independent and living life on my own terms, and partially because, although most guys I met thought I was an "amazing" girl, they just weren't that *into* me.

It was the most irritating thing in the world! *If I was so amazing, why didn't you want to date me?*

Instead of being the high powered CEO I always thought I'd be, I was living at home, with no company or business that would even let me get their coffee. I never thought once that my fantasy would not materialize, but sitting there, it felt exactly like what it was—a dream. Perspective changed everything.

I finished my pizza, wishing for more. I wasn't still hungry, considering I wasn't hungry when I started devouring the pizza. I just enjoyed the *taste* and it gave me an excuse to avoid another conversation about my job situation.

My phone was on silent, and I had forgotten it was even there until I saw the red light blinking. When I looked, there were two new text messages. The first was from my mom.

Mom: 3:25 pm: Are you home for dinner? Any ideas?

I was just formulating a lie I would tell my parents about not being home for dinner… until I realized I had told Rachel about the date. I would swear her to secrecy later. My parents were already on my case about finding a job, so I didn't want them to think that sharing even a little meant the lines for "relationship discussions" were open, because they most definitely were not!

The second text was from the cute guy from Wegman's. Seeing "Wegman's" associated with his name creeped me out. I still didn't know his name, and I couldn't think of a subtle way to ask.

I was way too awkward to just be blunt about the whole name thing. I decided the best solution to the name problem was to avoid it until we got married and the priest said "Do you, cute Wegman's guy, take Chelsea to be your wife?" assuming his birth name *wasn't* "Cute Wegman's guy."

> **Cute Wegman's Guy 3:27 pm:** Hope you slept well last night. I've heard Firebirds Happy Hour is best on rainy days. Hope to see you there. My name's Ben, by the way.

That was the *second* time he was able to read my mind via text message energy, so I couldn't decide if it was really cute or *stalker-turned-serial killer* creepy. I went with cute. The dating pool of twenty-something men in the NJ suburbs was so slim that I couldn't be picky, after all.

> **3:29 pm:** I think I can fit you into my schedule, five o'clock, right?

> **Cute Wegman's Guy 3:30 pm:** I'll be there.

Returning my gaze to the T.V. I saw my phone light up. Bridget was calling.
"Hey."
"Hey, I'm coming over. I'm so bored."
Five minutes later, she rang the doorbell.
"Wanna go jump on the trampoline?"
"No, but I'll sit on it while you jump."
"Fine."
My family has had a trampoline in my backyard for as long as I can remember. I'm not

even sure why, but the kids in the neighborhood used it more than any of us did. Still, it stayed.

The trampoline was already warm from the sun by the time we sat, letting our bodies rise and fall as it rippled with our movement.

"So anything happen since I last saw you?" she asked as she bounced on her knees.

"You mean with Chris? No, not really."

She looked at me with a face that said she knew there was more to it.

"I mean, he texted me again, but I don't know. It feels weird. We already *talked* about this. Remember?"

"Yeah, I remember. I just didn't know if you cracked or not yet."

My eyebrows furrowed and my mouth tilted up at one side.

"What does *that* mean?"

"Nothing. It's just... and we all do it, so don't think it's just you, but we all talk about how we don't even like these guys anymore and how we aren't going to respond, but then we all do. So I was just wondering if you'd given in yet."

"Uh okay, but this isn't really like you or Kenzie's situation. It's not like I keep going back to him. This is the first time we've talked in basically a year, so I'm not really sure why you're bringing this up."

"I'm just saying if you want to start talking to him again, we won't judge you or anything."

"Okay, but I don't want to."

She smiled and half-rolled her eyes. We both knew I was lying, the truth was I wanted to talk to him. I wanted to be with him, and it wasn't the pain of the heartbreak keeping me from giving in. It was the chance I'd look stupid again.

Women could survive heartbreak. Sadness could be overcome, but letting a guy fool you into falling for him again was a pain that most of us couldn't survive. No, I wouldn't let him make me feel that stupid again.

"Don't you have a date tonight? With that guy from Wegman's?"

Bridget's voice relieved the tension. Fortunately, our friendship had a two second bounce back rate.

"Yeah. I guess I should go get ready. We're supposed to meet at five."

"Are you excited?"

"I think I'm more nauseous."

"Yeah, I hate dates," she laughed. "I've never been on one that wasn't awkward, and I'm always scared the guy isn't going to be as cute as I remember."

"That's what I'm thinking!"

My face lit up. In a world that made me constantly question myself, it was nice having friends that made me feel like I belonged.

"I can't even remember what he looks like. What if I don't recognize him?"

"And then you have to ask the hostess and he's sitting right in front? That'd be so funny."

"Okay, no it wouldn't."

"Maybe I should come *with* you? Kenzie and Ashley can come too. We can sit at another table."

"Definitely not."

It took twenty minutes of back and forth mindless bickering to convince her she wasn't going.

I decided I would wear a loose, black tank top with a long gold necklace and ripped jean capris. I liked the dual purpose that the black tank top served, because black was slimming and the looseness of the tank top would hide the food baby that drinking and eating inevitably created.

I piled on every piece of makeup that I owned, which was ironic, because I was trying to go for the "au-naturale" look. I spent more time and used more makeup on not trying than I did when I tried to look like I tried. This whole makeup business was up there with electricity on the list of things I didn't understand about the world.

I looked in the mirror one last time, shoved my eyeliner, mascara, blush, and lip gloss into my teal satchel, just a few things in case I went to the bathroom during the night and decided I wasn't wearing enough makeup. As I headed downstairs I saw my Mom in the kitchen, I realized I needed an alibi.

"Rachel tells me you have a *date* tonight! That's exciting! Have fun."

I wished I hadn't said anything to Rachel. Now my Mom was excited for me to finally get a boyfriend and would ask me about him until I had to say it just didn't work out.

"Yup. Well, I gotta go."

"Don't forget to listen to what he says. Don't just talk about yourself. People like when other people are interested in someone other than themselves."

"But what if I'm not interested in *him*?"

"Well, Chelsea, then you should *pretend*, because you agreed to go out with him, and you need to be polite."

"Okay, I need to *leave!*"

"Don't eat anything stringy! You don't want cheese stuck on your chin all night." She called after me.

"I'll *definitely* keep that in mind, Mom. Bye."

I basically ran out of the house and headed across the dark garage to the door that led outside.

In the sheer excitement of "potentially *not* dying alone in an apartment and being eaten by cats," I forgot it was raining, which put me on a dead sprint to my car. I opened the door to my white two-door convertible and jumped in faster than Rose could jump off the lifeboat and back onto the *Titanic*.

Taking a glance in my rearview mirror, I noticed my hair, which I'd just spent time curling had already started to frizz from the humidity and misty rain. Grabbing the band off my wrist, I threw my hair into a bun—this would have to work, because there was no way I was going back into the house to another etiquette lesson!

I headed to Firebirds, changing the radio at least 50 times in the fifteen minutes it took for me to get there. I needed a song that would get me from the depressed "I hate everyone" mood I'd been in the last few days to in a girly, flirtatious mood. I hadn't felt so nervous in a long time. My hands were shaking as I switched gears.

Chapter 6

The First Date

As I pulled into the mall parking lot, I suddenly realized that I might not *recognize* Ben. I saw his face for what—a minute and a half? What if I completely walked past him? It was a big restaurant, and it's not like I could text him and tell him I was there, because he could be sitting right in front of me. *Well, it was official— the date was doomed!* I thought about going home, but I needed to face my fear and just hope I got there before he did—so he would have to be the one to have to recognize me.

The rain still hadn't stopped, so I ran toward the restaurant, making sure to do my best long stride model run, in case he could see me through the glass windows. In reality, I looked like a mole fleeing to its underground home.

I gave myself a little pep talk, raked my fingers through my hair and strode into the restaurant. I scanned the room. Fortunately I'd been there for Happy Hour before, so I knew if he wanted to do Happy Hour, then he could only be in the bar area, or on the porch.

Once I walked in, I saw him sitting against the back wall, at the table to the left of the fireplace. His brown hair looked like it was freshly buzzed and the maroon cotton t-shirt he wore accentuated his arms. He was wearing dark jeans, and for some bizarre reason, the fireplace was going, even though it was summer.

I guess the restaurant really wanted to set the mood for the special occasion. All I could think as I walked towards him was about how hot he must be. He was probably regretting wearing the maroon shirt, which would inevitably leave *sweat stains*. He was much cuter in his civilian clothes than in that green Wegman's apron! My "neurotic" form of nervousness changed into a more "excited" form for the first time since I left the house. My hands stopped shaking.

I was closing in on the table, about five feet away, I reminded myself to smile. Before I knew it, I was there, and the date had officially begun. *What is he doing? Why is he getting up? Are we going somewhere?* Then I realized that he was getting up to hug me.

"Hey, what's up? Sorry I'm late."

"Yeah, no problem. I just got here a few minutes ago. The menu looks good. Do you want to get some food, or just drinks?"

Well that depends, are you buying? Because I hadn't yet applied for unemployment my income was minimal, *like $0 minimal*. I hated this part about a date, or at least I *imagined* I hated this part about a date. I was expecting him to pay, which meant that I should probably answer that *I didn't need food*—even though I was *starving*! It also meant I should get a $2 beer instead of a $5 cocktail, even though I didn't particularly enjoy beer. I always wondered if guys spent as much time analyzing situations as girls did.

As he pulled out my chair and I sat, I knew I had to come up with an appropriate answer, quickly. *Why couldn't my mom have told me anything about what to do when he asks if you want food, or just drinks?*

"I *could* eat, but their drinks here are really good, too. I recommend the cucumber gimlet."

Good idea, Chelsea—recommend a drink so he'll get the hint you want a $5 drink instead of a $2 beer!

"Well, *I'm* gonna have a beer, but I'll get *you* one of those."

Oh, you'll get me one of those? Are you going to go behind the bar and mix my drink then walk it over to me? Am I going to tip you afterwards? Instead of acknowledging that he was attempting to be a gentleman, I was insulting him. *This is why I don't go on dates!*

After the waitress came over, he ordered the drinks. Just then, I began to get that nauseous feeling that came on when I hadn't eaten for a while. I thought to Google how late the food court was open—so I could get something to eat after the date was over. I was feeling light-headed when he broke the silence.

"I was thinking the pigs-in-a-blanket and the pretzels and beer cheese? Sorry—I'm just really hungry. I haven't eaten since this morning."

I could hear the angels singing! What a good man! Women will never admit it, but similar to men, the way to our hearts is through our stomachs—except for maybe the Victoria's Secret models. The way to their hearts is through treadmills and carrot sticks. Maybe I wouldn't have to go to the food court after all.

"I'm so glad you said that, because I'm hungry too, but I didn't know if you ate already, so I didn't want to assume we were getting food if you just wanted to get drinks... and we'd only been sitting here for like, two minutes, so I didn't want to rush into appetizers..." My voice was racing, I was talking way too fast.

The waitress brought the drinks and when she asked if we were ready to order food. Momentarily forgetting that I was on a date, I jumped right in.

"Yeah! Actually, we'll have the pigs in the blanket and the pretzels. Thanks so much!"

I handed her our menus and she walked away. Taking a sip of my drink, I looked across the table, realizing I was there with a *guy*, and not just one of my friends!

"Oh, shit! I'm sorry! Was it weird I just ordered?"

This was going well...

He laughed, which made me laugh as well.

"No, it's fine. I mean, I *usually* do the ordering, but you *rocked* it. I think you may actually have a career in doing it."

Well, maybe it was going well, and not in a sarcastic way either.

"Yeah maybe if my designs don't work out I'll become a professional food orderer."

I made sure to giggle so he knew I wasn't mocking him. As I took another sip of my drink, I casually glanced at his beer, which was still almost full. I didn't want to be slugging down drinks if he was casually sipping. That was the other thing about dates—it was necessary to gauge the timing so that both people finished eating and drinking at the same time. Otherwise, there was that risk of looking like a pig eating at a trough.

"Oh you're a designer?"

"Yeah, I mean I guess. They haven't been picked up by any stores yet, so I guess it's actually more of a hobby."

"Just because you aren't getting paid to do it doesn't make you any less a designer. People call themselves runners all the time, and I'm pretty positive the moms in my town aren't getting paid to do it. Do you want another drink?"

He made so much sense. I started to think I actually liked him. And to think this whole time he'd been hiding in the produce section of the grocery store. I'd barely noticed I'd finished my entire drink until he asked if I wanted a second. Was it rude to order two?

As the server delivered the appetizers, he took a long drag on his beer and answered for both of us.

"We'll have another round, whenever you get a chance."

I immediately decided I liked him. I mean, what was *not* to like about a guy who enjoyed taking advantage of half-priced drinks?

"So what do *you* do? I mean, *besides* carrots and celery..."

"I'm actually going to medical school, but I really enjoy doing stand-up comedy. I've had some minor success, but for some reason, I haven't become a millionaire yet. Wegman's pays the bills."

"So you agree? You think you're really *funny?*"

I knew *Mean Girls* would come in handy one day. He laughed and took a sip of his beer.

Meanwhile, I was sending Tina Fey a thank you note in my mind.

For the next two rounds, the conversation flowed effortlessly. We went together better than Sandy and Danny, and for a few minutes, I thought I'd found a soul mate. That was until he said...

"So, why don't you have a *boyfriend?*"

I looked at him, puzzled. *Did I hear him right, or was I just drunker than I thought?* That was a question that it just made no sense to ask anyone—*ever!* I was tempted to be uncomfortably honest and put it all out there.

Well—my last boyfriend told me I was a psycho, even though I very consciously tried to be normal most of the time. A lot of guys think I'm amazing, but they don't want to date me, and I guess the fact that I haven't been to the gym in ages and our society's superficiality play into it too. Long story short—no one has wanted to date me until this point. So how about you?

The "so why don't you have a boyfriend?" question was like when people asked "How are you?" It's a question that, under no circumstances, anyone is expected to answer honestly. Instead, I decided to go with the socially acceptable answer.

"Oh, I don't know. I guess I just haven't found anyone *special* yet."

Talk about a conversation killer! Saying I hadn't found anyone *special* yet was code for "I've dated losers who eventually *dumped* me."

"Yeah, I *feel* that. I had a really serious relationship a few months back, but she broke up with me and I felt really bad about it... until I found out she had a new *girlfriend*."

I accidentally coughed a sip of my drink back out into the martini glass.

"I'm *sorry?* Did you say she had another *girlfriend?*"

I needed confirmation for what I heard. I mean, I had four drinks—so it was possible I misheard what he said.

"Yeah, after that, I didn't feel so bad about myself anymore."

Since I knew he did stand-up comedy, I refused to react, waiting for him to laugh and tell me he was joking. He didn't.

"Well, *that* seems traumatizing. Seeing a therapist about it?"

It was my Hail Mary pass—calling him out on the apparent joke.

"I did, *actually.*"

Okay—not a joke. Wow, the conversation was going downhill fast! There was no escaping the awkwardness that hovered there. I was on the Titanic—with no lifeboats. All I could do was watch it sink. *Then it got worse!*

"Honestly, I don't believe in monogamous relationships. I feel they're so old-fashioned, and it's human behavior for men to be interested in many women."

I sat in silence, sipping my drink. All hopes that he was joking were dying faster than the goldfish won at the state fair.

The waitress broke the silence.

"So, are we gonna do another round, or are you guys *good?*"

She clearly hadn't *heard* the conversation. We were definitely *not* getting another round. I was regretting the first four!

"You know—I have to get *home*. It's kind of late, and I have to be up early."

He didn't know me that well, so he didn't know I didn't have to get up at any specific time at any time the foreseeable future.

"You *sure*?" He stared at me, I looked down. "Okay, can you just bring us the check?"

Yes, I'm sure! Were we not on the same date? And what was this "bring us the check?" I thought sitting through that date from hell warranted me a free meal and a few free drinks.

When the waitress brought the check a few minutes later, I made the obligatory move towards my purse—slow enough to allow him time to stop me, though making just enough effort to make him *think* I actually was fine splitting the check...

"No. Don't worry. I got it."

Jackpot! After that conversation, I deserved it.

"Oh, are you *sure*? I don't mind."

"Yeah, don't worry about it. Put your wallet away."

Great! I was up a free dinner and a severe case of dating PTSD, but just as I was about to get up and leave, he stopped me.

"So uh, what's your favorite *time* to eat dinner?"

That last question sealed the deal! It was officially the worst date ever. The date had gone so far downhill that I could barely manage a fake giggle, much less a response. I just smiled and pretended to text someone. *How people survived awkward encounters before the invention of cell phones was beyond me!*

After we got up and walked toward the door, I rummaged through my purse for the keys.

"I'm parked on the other side, but I had a great time. We should do it *again*."

"Yeah, for sure. I had a lot of fun. Thanks again for dinner."

Whether he was being funny or just being polite, we were one hundred percent *not* going to do it again! I smiled and gave him the obligatory side hug before turning away.

One of the most common lies ever spoken in the human language was the "let's do it again sometime," which was nearly as common as the "No—those horizontal stripes don't make you look fat at all" falsehood.

It was still raining so I ran through the parking lot, still rummaging for my keys. When I finally reached my car, my heart racing from that sprint, I found my keys, only they weren't in my purse—they were on the front seat of my car, and all the doors were locked! Standing in the rain, I texted the first person who came to mind—my sister, Rachel.

> 10:15 pm: I locked my keys in the car. Can you come get me I'm at Firebirds?
> Rachel: 10:16 pm: Yea. I guess the date went well. You've been there for five hours.

> 10:17 pm: It went about as well as Watergate. I'll tell you in the car.

I was going to be there for a while, so I walked back towards the mall entrance, hoping escape the rain. I reached for the door, when just my luck, I was met with disappointment—the door was locked and there was no awning for cover, so I sat on the curb in the pouring rain, waiting for my sister.

As I got drenched, I prayed Ben wouldn't drive past and see me. Having to endure a fifteen minute car ride home with him would be just the icing on top of the date from hell cake. My sister arrived in her white Jetta fifteen minutes later. After I got in and buckled my seatbelt, I told her about the night, down to every last awkward detail.

As I shared my story, I realized that, only a few short hours earlier, I felt happier than I had in a while. The next thing I knew, I was sitting on a curb in the rain, wondering what I would put as my interests on Match.com. There it was—the whole perspective thing again.

"Well, at *least* you got a free meal out of it! Right?"

"Rachel, not even a free lobster and filet mignon meal would have been worth the date I just had!"

Chapter 7

The Ghost of Boyfriends Past

My mom's voice woke me up at 9:30 on Thursday morning.

"You need to clean your room for the cleaners they're coming in about an hour." She turned on my light as she spoke.

"Mom, it's so early!"

I threw a pillow over my face.

"Chelsea, it's ten. Don't act like I came in here at the crack of dawn."

I groaned and rolled over onto my stomach, face down in my mattress.

"If you're going to live here you're going to live by our rules. Now please clean your rom." She said as she closed the door behind her, leaving the light on.

If I was going to live here? She said it like this was some fantasy island that I was choosing to stay on. Being 22 and living at home wasn't exactly how I pictured my life, I wouldn't be here if I had another choice.

I looked at my phone and saw a text from Ben.

Ben: 8:35 am: "Hey. I hope you slept well. I had a lot of fun last night."

The memories of the previous night came flooding back to me at once. Dropping the phone, I collapsed onto the pillow. I would respond to his text later, or maybe never. I didn't want to go out with him ever again, but I also really didn't like hurting people's feelings. The only way I could rid myself of the uneasy feeling in my stomach was to not respond. Oh, and I'd have to find a new grocery store to eliminate any future encounters.

As I rolled out of bed, I caught a glimpse of my bedroom floor. If the memories of the previous night weren't bad enough, the memories of Monday morning's battle with my closet lied on the ground before of me. I grabbed a pair of black leggings off the floor and put them on. A black tank dress would serve as a shirt. Sure, I may have looked like I belonged on TLC's *Breaking Amish*, but it was comfortable and meant there were two fewer things I had to put away before the cleaners arrived.

I stumbled to the bathroom, and after taking a glance in the mirror, I decided it would be one of those "no makeup" days. For each day of the week, I got progressively worse looking. That's why I always planned job interviews on Mondays. Well, *hypothetically* I planned job interviews on Mondays. I hadn't actually had a job interview since I was 16, when I was forced to earn a living making minimum wage at Coldstone Creamery.

As much as I wanted to rebel against the rules my parents set for me and take a stand against how unfair the world was, I also didn't want to be homeless so, I sat on the ground and started to fold my clothes. I folded four shirts and two pairs of pants, bringing them to their proper drawers. As I closed the drawers and turned around I noticed an absurd amount of clothes still on the ground, this could take all morning and I had plans. I made a choice and did the only responsible thing an adult can do in this situation, I grabbed all of the clothes off the ground and threw them into the boxes that covered one corner of my room.

As soon as I opened my bedroom door to head downstairs I heard;

"Chelsea do *not* just throw all of those clothes back into the boxes. It's time to put them away!"

That was the one problem with moms—they knew *everything*!

I left the clothes where they were in the boxes in the corner of my room and headed downstairs. I was emotionally traumatized from the events of last night and deserved a personal day, from my extended string of personal days.

In college, I rebelled against the bureaucracy that surrounded the university lifestyle by occasionally turning in assignments late, but back at home, the inner rebel in me found pleasure in leaving the clothes where they were. I knew my mom would probably never know the secret rebellion I planned, and in the grand scheme of things, *I* probably wouldn't remember it—but I needed to feel like I was making a difference, at least for a few seconds.

As I headed downstairs, I smelled pork roll frying in the skillet. Pork roll was the king of all breakfast meats, and it eased my depression about living at home, since it was not available outside New Jersey. Some people thought of New Jersey as a trash heap, but there's no way a state true to their stereotypes could produce such a wonderful breakfast food, or Bruce Springsteen.

"What are you making?"

It was obvious what Rachel was making, but it sounded nicer than just coming out and demanding that she make me one as well.

"Pork roll, egg and cheese."

"Oh, yum! *I'll* have one of those, please."

If I was going to be stuck living at home, I was at least going to get some breakfast out of it.

"Fine."

Well, I didn't expect our conversation to go so smoothly. I expected her to at least put up a fight. She was getting soft at the ripe old age of 24. By the time she turned 80, she'd be practically giving me the Louis Vuitton bag she bought in Paris last spring.

"Are you excited for your party?"

"Yeah, I think it'll be fun. Plus, I could really *use* the cash. As good as this whole brooding, impoverished designer lifestyle is going, I wouldn't mind being able to move out before 45."

I knew it was wrong to *expect* people to bring money, but I figured that, if people could have housewarming parties so they could later open gifts filled with things to fill their new home, I could have a graduation party to fill my unemployed bank account. Plus, I had actually *accomplished* something. All a house warming party celebrates is a swipe of the credit card.

"I think I got a few thousand at mine. It's really nice to have that money—especially since you don't have a job lined up yet. Isn't that the whole point of having a graduation party?"

Great minds think alike. Maybe we were more alike, after all. Sure, we didn't see eye to eye on most things, but where it counted—like milking our relatives for pity money—we agreed.

Throughout my years of growth at college I'd realized how small my world had been. None of my friends had divorced parents growing up, at least not until we were almost out of high school. It wasn't until I went to school that I realized "normal" families were rare and I was lucky to have mine. Sure we fought, sometimes I was even worried it'd be the breaking point but we always seemed to find our way back together. I think my parents were responsible for most of that, and I'd be lying if I said I wasn't worried that without them we'd dismantle.

Our lives were now going in different directions and getting together for a simple Sunday dinner could no longer have a mandatory attendance rule. Without many significant romantic relationships it sometimes felt like my family was all I had and whenever I felt any of those relationships were broken, my Mom would remind me it'd all be fine. Even small moments like these, when Rachel and I agreed on even something so minor, it made me believe that we'd be fine.

When I heard my mom walk into the kitchen, I prayed she wouldn't ask about the date, even though I knew she would.

"Chelsea! How was your date? You got home pretty late. I just hope you didn't drink too much to drive last night. I don't know why kids your age feel you need to drink in such *excessive* amounts!"

I glared at Rachel from across the kitchen.

"You *told* her!"

"No I didn't. I told her your keys got locked inside your car, but she didn't *believe* me. You're welcome for going and getting your car this morning, by the way."

"Chelsea—do not blame your binge drinking on your sister. Now, *tell* me about the date!"

"I did *not* binge drink! I actually was stuck waiting outside in the rain because my keys were locked in my car, so you should feel pretty bad about it. And the date was terrible. Thanks for asking."

"What? Terrible? Why?"

"He was weird. I really don't want to go into details, Mom. It was just weird, and I'm never going back to Wegman's again."

She was persistent on the issue of boyfriends.

"You should give him a chance. Maybe he was just *nervous*…"

"No. He's weird. The date was terrible, and I'm definitely *not* giving him another chance. Can we talk about something *else* now?"

"I just don't know how girls could not want a *boyfriend*. I can remember when I was your age— the only thing I wanted was a boyfriend, and when I was in a relationship, I only really wanted to be around that person. It's just so *different* today!"

My sister had always had a boyfriend, and as my mom grew older, she became more conservative—something I think is normal with women as they grow older. They yearn for their younger days as a way to defy the fact that they're getting older.

Whatever it was, my mother and sister wouldn't get off my back about relationships. They didn't understand why any woman would want to be single, while I didn't understand how any woman would want to be tied down to a man without first accomplishing everything she wanted out of life.

I could never be that other type of woman, no matter how hard I tried. There was so much I wanted from life, and a relationship meant passing up opportunities and downsizing my dreams, which I couldn't afford, even if it meant I might end up alone.

"I know the two of you think having a boyfriend is the single most important thing in the world, but believe it or not, I don't *want* a boyfriend. I want to be able to go wherever I want and take advantage of whatever opportunities that come my way, no matter what. I only want to worry about one person's opinion, and that person is mine."

"Whoa! You're being sensitive."

I hated when Rachel told me I was being sensitive—as if I wasn't allowed to exist without people being on my case about every little thing.

"Chelsea—I don't think having a boyfriend is the *most* important thing. I'm just saying that, for me and your sister..."

"Okay! Whatever! I don't want to talk about this anymore."

I stared at my empty plate and held back what I'd wanted to say every time this conversation came up. It wasn't that women didn't want boyfriends, that *I* didn't want one. Yes, I was worried if I was in a relationship I wouldn't just pack up and move wherever and whenever I got the chance but that wasn't it, not really. I didn't have the heart to tell them that the real reason I didn't have a boyfriend was because every time I let myself get close to someone they realized I wasn't the one.

An awesome girl, sure, but not the one they saw themselves with. Guys didn't want girls who were sarcastic and smart and independent. They wanted blonde hair, big boobs and a six pack, girls who didn't care what they did or how they treated them. I'd tried for a while to be one of those girls but it just wasn't me and I'd realized I'd rather be alone than pretend.

When I heard my text ringtone, I assumed it was Ben, inviting me on yet another episode of *Punk'd: Dating Edition*.

Chris: 9:25 am: Listen, I know you don't want to talk to me, and I get that, but after everything that's happened between us, I never thought you'd treat me like this. I really want to see you!

I couldn't decide if I was angry that he was trying to make me feel guilty about not responding to his text after everything he had done to me, or if I was just glad that the person I had wanted for so long finally wanted me back. Either way, I had to get out of that house.

"Thanks for breakfast. I'm actually gonna head to Starbuck's. I need to get some work done on my pieces and I can't think here."

"You're *really* not going to finish that?"

The fact that Rachel was surprised I was leaving food on my plate made me momentarily question my eating habits—and by "momentarily," I meant a split-second.

"I'm not hungry anymore."

Those were words I never thought I would say, but then again, I never thought I would be living at home, with such a bleak future. I shoved my sketchbook in my bag and headed down the hallway toward the garage. I made it fifteen feet down the hallway before turning around, grabbing the remains of my breakfast and continuing on my way.

I decided that, while Chris could take away my desire to be in any relationship ever again, and while he could ruin all my memories from last summer, he could never take away my love for eating. Plus, I never fully understood how life events—especially breakups—could put people off their appetites. Food was instant gratification and if it ever disappointed, you could just eat something *else*. Food always ended on a good note—except Chinese food, where people usually ended up on couches groaning about how much they ate.

After realizing I couldn't simultaneously drive and eat, I shoved the last few bites of my breakfast into my mouth and off I went. As I drove, I felt my phone burning a hole in my purse and my heart. I had taken a vow not to text while driving after a friend of my sister had been in a traumatic car accident. The only thing worse than texting and driving was emotional texting and driving, which I was.

Part of me wanted to forget him and move on, but the rest of me, the bigger part of me, couldn't deny that he'd been my first love, and that, for months, I'd been hoping to hear the exact words he was saying to me. That *had* to count for something, right? My mind was reeling as I made the ten-minute drive to the local Starbucks.

I passed all of the familiar houses and landmarks—places I'd passed for the past 22 years—and it finally hit me that, if life kept going at the rate it was going, I'd be a lifer. I had the same feeling before I left for college—the feeling that you'd spontaneously combust if you didn't get out soon—but I had no idea about *how* I was going to get out, if ever.

I put the car in park, pulled up on the emergency break, grabbed my bag and headed inside. With every step I took on the black asphalt parking lot, I felt my heart sink lower into my stomach. Suddenly I missed the days when I sat around, wishing every new text was from him. It seemed easier back then.

I put my bag down on a wooden chair at a two-person table in the middle of the room, securing my spot before getting my drink. I was waiting for my drink to be called when, from the corner of my eye, I saw someone coming towards me. It was Drew, one of my oldest friends.

We were really close in high school… well, as close as a girl and boy can be without leaving the *friend zone*. We had formed one of those friendships depicted in the movies—best friends, connected on a level that came with an air of comfort whenever we were together. There was a time when I thought I had feelings for him, but *unlike* in the movies, he never had a similar epiphany. I kept my feelings to myself.

After we went to college, our mindsets changed and we each found replacement friends, so we kinda drifted apart. He went to school on the East Coast, I went to school on the West Coast and by the time I was coming back East he was headed out West. Still, whenever I saw him I could feel my heart skip just a few beats.

"Hey, Chelsea! Haven't seen you in forever!"

His smile started to melt the ice that had formed around my heart since Chris, it was good to see him, surprising but good.

"Yeah I know it's been a while. Wait, what are you doing home? Aren't you supposed to be in California?"

"I moved back, actually. That lifestyle wasn't really for me. Thankfully, the investment firm I was with had an opening out here in Philly, so I jumped at the chance."

He moved back? When? Suddenly, I felt angry, hurt. We used to be so close, but I wasn't even on his list of people to tell that he's in town?

"Oh, when?"

I tried to hide the shock in my voice.

"About a month ago? Maybe more?"

I nodded, it was the only movement I could make.

"So what's going on with you?"

"Me? Oh the usual, just hanging out at home, working on some designs. I actually just got back a few days ago."

"That's awesome. I'm real excited for your party."

"Oh? You're coming?"

"Well, you invited me, or at least someone did on Facebook."

"Yeah, I just didn't even realize you were in town, since I didn't know you lived here now."

I could tell what I said cut a cord somewhere inside him—*what* cord, I didn't know. It was ridiculous I was even upset about it, yes we'd been close once, what? Four years ago? We'd barely spoken in the last two.

"I mean, I don't *have* to come."

He looked down at the floor, fiddling with the straw in his drink.

"No. Come, really. I guess I was just surprised to see you. Seriously, *come!*."

I smiled and shook my head, trying to lighten the mood.

"Fine. Fine, if you're going to beg me to."

His hand grazed my arm.

"Can I actually bring someone? I'm kind of dating this girl, and she's new to Philly, so I think it'd be cool if you guys could be friends."

After practically abandoning our friendship and not even telling me he was in town, he wanted to bring a random girl to my party?

"Yeah, of course. It's casual anyways."

Please!   It's not like I could say "no."

"Great, I'll see you then," he said as he walked towards the door.

A few feet from the door, he turned around.

"You look good, by the way. And just keep trying. Your designs are good. Fuck anyone who doesn't think so."

He smiled and walked out the door.

Something about him was different. Maybe California had made him less uptight, a little more confident? I couldn't tell if it was seeing him for the first time in a while or true emotions, but something made my heart beat a little faster.

I grabbed my drink and I sat at the wooden table, catching a final glimpse of him walking away. His brown hair crowned a slightly tall, medium build body. I finally understood—we were adults, so the childish love games we played in our youth were behind us.

Maybe any hope of a future for us was also in the past. My nostalgia gave way to anger. If he was *really* my friend, why didn't he tell me he was in town? He knew I had moved back home, so he should have known I would be bored and would want to do something. He was a *terrible* friend!

I opened my sketchbook and stared at the pages containing my life's work as I reached for my phone. I know breathing is involuntary, but I now had hard evidence that emotional texting was an involuntary behavior too. My fingers were typing out words without my brain even telling them to do so. What remained was a single message to Chris.

10:00 am: I know. I want to see you, too.

I'm not sure it was the romantic adrenaline rush I felt after seeing Drew, or maybe it was because my heart knew something my head didn't. Whatever it was, I felt motivated to press send. As I put my phone down on the table, I regretted that I had given in to his seriously *minor* gesture of reconciliation, but I felt the most intense feeling of satisfaction. Sometimes making a decision—even if it's the wrong one—gives us just the relief we need.

I plugged my headphones into my iPod, trying to get some sort of inspiration. I drew and tweaked my drawings for hours but it felt like no time had passed, I could have probably worked longer if it wasn't for the 18 something year old boy who clearly never learned that headphones in meant conversation out.

I looked up briefly from the colored pages—one split-second glance that would seal my fate. I saw him looking at me and saw his mouth moving, but couldn't hear what he was saying over the music on my headphones. Following the social grace for headphone encounters, I removed the headphones.

"I'm sorry—*what* did you say? I had my headphones on."

Employing the same subtlety of attitude I used with my parents, I used just enough attitude to make sure he got the idea that I was annoyed, but not enough to get me into trouble.

I always thought that having headphones on made it obvious that a person could not hear someone talking to them, but it wouldn't have been the first time I thought something was obvious to the world, when it wasn't.

"Oh, yeah—I was just wondering if someone was *sitting* here…"

I took a quick glance around the room, counting one, two, three, four—four open tables, and he wanted to sit at *mine*?

"Uh, no. Go ahead."

I moved my pages closer to me and took my bag off the chair. Inviting him to sit down at my small, round table when there were at least four other tables available was like inviting a friend you didn't really *like* to your party. The invitation was a courtesy, but the entire time, you're hoping they won't come.

I put my headphones back in, as they were my only defense against unwanted conversation, and I managed to get half of a shoe done before, from the corner of my eye, I saw his mouth moving again. I took the headphones off again.

"What?"

"Oh, sorry—I was just wondering what your drink is. It looks good."

By that point, I had been sipping my chai latte long enough that it was at the 99% melted ice/ 1% chai latte stage—where it formed a nice cloudy white color. Far from looking good, it looked disgusting!

"Chai latte."

My ear buds went back in, as he had already exceeded his allotted conversation time. This time I got one shoe done before I noticed him staring at me. I removed the headphones, but I kept them close enough that I could pop them right back in after I answered whatever inane question he was going to ask.

"What are you *working* on?"

"Nothing!"

If I was going to finish enough pieces for a presentation before my five-year high school reunion, I didn't have time for his annoying questions.

"It looks like you're working on *something*."

"Okay. Yeah, I'm working on a fashion line, and I'd appreciate it if I could work *quietly.*"

"Oh! So you're a designer? Where would I have seen your stuff?"

Where did this kid get off disrupting me like this?

"Uh, yeah. I guess. And nowhere, I guess it's actually just a hobby."

With that, I put my headphones on, maxed out the volume and managed to get a whole two pairs of pants done before I couldn't endure his staring any longer and decided to leave. I packed up my stuff as quickly as I could, leaving no room for any more of his small talk.

"It was nice meeting you."

"Yeah you too, good luck on your... uh... chemistry homework."

I added a little personal touch to my goodbye, since we had spent such a lovely twenty minutes together. Making my way toward the door, I grabbed my sunglasses from the dark abyss in my bag in time before I reached the outside world.

Being the gifted multi-tasker, I checked my phone as I walked toward my car in the parking lot. A single red dot stared me in the face, and as I opened up my text messages, I just stared at my phone, conjuring up all sorts of responses that Chris would have for me. The message I saw was something I never expected.

Mom: 4:30 pm: Are you going to be home for dinner? We're planning on going to sushi.

Thanks, Mom, and yes—I'd be home for dinner. Where *else* would I be? I hope she didn't really expect me to go out with that guy from Wegman's again! I didn't care how much she wanted grandchildren. I was not suffering through *that* again!

As I informed my mom of my dinner desires, I noticed I had no other messages—no message from Chris, no love text from Drew, saying he couldn't stop thinking about me— nothing. I immediately began to regret my decision to respond. The immense satisfaction I felt hours earlier was replaced by anxiety that surrounded my life. Had I given in too soon? Was he rethinking how he felt? Was I going down the same road I went down the previous summer? I knew one thing for certain—love made psychos of us all.

I made it halfway home before a truly awful song came on and I was forced to change the radio. Passing through the first three preset channels, I settled on the fourth, and as I looked into my rearview mirror, I noticed something odd—red and blue flashing lights. I turned the steering wheel slightly to the right and pulled onto the shoulder. Once I was safely on the side of the road, I put the car in park, rolled down the window and reached for my wallet.

"You have got to be fucking kidding me!"

Unfortunately, this police officer was the young-and-in-shape type, and not the fat-donut-eating type, so by the time I was able to grab my wallet and mumble to myself, he was already at my window. I turned and smiled—the only thing I could do.

"Do you know that your left tail light is out?"

I wanted to say, *Well no, sir. I did not know that—considering my talents don't include a sixth-sense for burned-out tail lights.*

"No. Is it? I'm sorry. I had no idea. I'll get it fixed right away."

"Yeah, you *should.* It can be pretty dangerous. Let me just run your information, and you can be on your way."

I gave him my license and registration, along with my best smile, and let him wander back to his vehicle. He seemed reasonable, and it's a good thing—because my *freelance designer's* paycheck couldn't pay for driving tickets. When I saw him coming back, I silently prepared my *thank you* speech.

"Everything looks good, so here's just the ticket for the tail light. As long as you pay it on time, there's no court date or points on your license or anything."

Excuse me? I stared at him longer than usual, a little confused as to why he was handing me a ticket.

"Awesome."

I added just enough sass in my voice to make sure he knew how annoyed I was and how ridiculous the ticket was, but not enough for him to give me a ticket for anything else.

"Listen, I'm kind of new around here, and I was just wondering if you might want to get a drink or something sometime."

"Are you *joking*?"

"No. I know it sounds weird after the whole ticket thing, but since I'm new, I can't really let people *off.* But I think you're very pretty, and I don't know a lot of people here, so I was hoping you might want to get to know each other sometime."

I could see *why* he didn't know a lot of people. He was probably older than me by a few years, but he was still incredibly attractive. His short, dirty blonde hair was perfectly side-swept across his face, and his deep, blue eyes and sun-tanned skin made me almost forget about the ticket... almost.

"Yeah, well I'm not really into dating right now. Sorry."

"Well, if you decide you want to *start* dating, here's my card. Or, if you have a need for your local law enforcement..."

I wanted to laugh, and had I been minus one driving ticket, I would have laughed.

"Isn't that what 9-1-1 is for?"

As he laughed, I saw dimples creep out from the corner of his smile.

"Have a nice day."

"Yeah, welcome to town."

I waited for him to walk back to his car before pulling away. I never understood tickets for broken tail lights. It wasn't the same as speeding or parking illegally, and there was no way drivers could ever know their tail lights were broken. They only found out when a police officer told them about it. It was similar to Great White Sharks, waiting on seals to leave their island. The police could just sit and wait, and eventually someone would come by with a burned-out taillight, completely unaware of the trap that was set for them.

It was all too much. I couldn't hold the emotion back any longer. I'd barely made it to the light before I felt the tears stream down my face. I couldn't go home crying. No one there would have understood what I was going through. I took my first left and headed down the street towards Kenzie's house.

"Hey, I'm at your house. Can you come outside?"

"Yeah. Wait—are you crying? Is everything okay?"

"No. Just come *out*."

"Okay, I'm coming. You're not... *pregnant*, are you?"

I managed a slight laugh through my tears.

"No, Kenzie. I am definitely *not* pregnant."

She opened the car door and got in.

"What happened? Is it Chris?"

"No. Yes. I don't know. It's just *everything*! I can't *take* it anymore."

"What do you mean?"

"I just never thought I'd *feel* like this, and I *hate* it. I have moments when I feel really good, and I am so positive, but they're minimal, and most of the time, I feel like there's something weighing me down—like I'm never going to do anything productive with my life—ever! And then I start crying, and it just gets worse."

As she sat staring at me for what seemed like forever, I worried that my friends didn't share my misery. I thought we were in it together, that what I was feeling was normal, but maybe it *wasn't*?

"No, I *understand*," she insisted. "It's so frustrating it that makes you want to scream, just so you'll be heard—so you feel like you're of some minor significance in this world. I get it. And everyone *acts* like they understand, and they try to give you advice, but none of it helps. Our *parents* don't understand what it's like. It was so *different* for them."

"I just wish someone would tell me if I have *real* talent, or just man-up and tell me it's time to throw in the towel and accept that I'm going to work a mindless job for the next 45 years!"

"Chels—*listen* to me. I've seen some of your stuff, mostly on your Instagram, but you *have* talent!"

I rolled my eyes.

"I'm *serious*! Don't give up yet. It'll *happen* for you. Trust me."

I wiped my nose on my shirt sleeve and took a deep breath.

"That is so disgusting," she complained. "Don't you have *napkins* in here?"

"No. I didn't think I was going to be moving to anyplace where I would need a car, but look where I am."

"Okay. Well, you're never going to get a job if you keep wiping your snot on your sleeve, so maybe invest in some napkins."

I tried to laugh it off, but the tears kept coming.

"What? Stop crying. It's gonna be *fine*."

Kenzie's supportive voice and words only made me cry more.

"I know, and I don't even know why I'm still crying, but it's just so hard all the time—with everything I do. I went to Firebirds with that guy from Wegman's yesterday, and it was so terrible

I never want to go on a date again, and then everything with Chris! I just don't understand why I can't seem to find a halfway *normal* guy who likes me!"

"Guys are such assholes! You really can't let that bother you so much. It's gonna all work out. Just give it time. But wait—tell me more about the date."

"Basically, it was going great until he told me he dated a girl who turned out to be a *lesbian*, and he went to a *therapist* about it."

All of a sudden, Kenzie was crying too—she was doubled over in the passenger seat, laughing hysterically, yet she was able to pose a question.

"Can you take a minute to think about what you just *said?*"

"I know. It was *so* bad! And then, just now I got a ticket for my stupid tail light, and then the cop asked me *out*."

As I looked over at her, we stared at each other in silence and broke out laughing. I guess sometimes, when all the crying's done, you just have to laugh.

I walked through my front door a little later as I opened up Instagram on my phone.

"Are you fucking *kidding* me?"

"*Chelsea Elizabeth!*"

The harshness in my mom's tone woke me from my social media daydream as I realized I had reacted by speaking much louder than I thought I had.

"I'm sorry, Mom, but look at this picture!"

I turned the phone toward my two sisters and mother, where they sat in the kitchen. I wanted them to see the horror I had just experienced.

"This girl posts a stupid picture of herself doing that thing—where you purse your lips so your cheeks get sucked in, and you look really skinny, even though you aren't—and guess what? She got 150 *likes* on it!"

Based on their faces, which lacked the sense of shock I anticipated, I could see they did not fully understand what I was saying. So I continued.

"It just doesn't make any sense! I posted a picture of my head in a paper mache shark's mouth, and *I* got 13 likes. So this girl posts a picture of her stupid face, and she gets 150?"

Still nothing? How were they *not* understanding the sense of social injustice I was experiencing? Obviously, my *resume* wasn't giving me any self-confidence boosters, so social media was the only other source of validation I had in my sad life.

"You know what? If people aren't even going to be grateful for my witty social media presence, why do I even *post* things? Everyone's so rude!"

"Chelsea," Sarah explained. "You aren't *that* funny. Even I get like 100 likes every time I post anything. You don't, because you don't have a lot of followers."

I felt immediately defensive after my sister's attempt at explaining reality.

"It's about the *ratio*, Sarah. If you follow a ton of people and a ton of people follow you, it doesn't *count*. *Anyone* can get people to follow them back. I don't follow a lot of people, which means that my ratio is *better* than yours.

"You're the only person who *thinks* that."

That was the thing about 18-year-olds—they thought they knew everything. At least when I was in college, I was able to tell her what was what in the world. Unemployed and facing a bleak future, I feared she'd remind me of that fact in every retort.

"Mom! Aren't you going to tell her to stop piling on? This is *ridiculous!* I say one thing, and it's like I just killed Bambi's mom, but then people can say whatever to me, and it's fine!"

"You're being so overdramatic," Sarah interjected. "Literally!"

"I'm going upstairs, and I'm *not* dramatic. I'm just passionate—about all aspects of my life, and I'd appreciate a little *sympathy!*"

I made it to the stairs before I heard my mom call after me.

"Your father will be home in an hour, and we're going to dinner."

I'd always wanted to be one of those kids that could refuse eating in order to punish the family for being mean or otherwise inconsiderate, but I never could. I was always too hungry.

When I got in my room, I slammed the door loud enough to let them to know I was definitely not over the mistreatment, but not hard enough to cause my mom yell at me about it. I wanted them to feel bad, but I did want listen to a forced lecture telling me that *if I didn't like the rules in that house, then I should move out...* considering I had no move-out money.

I flopped down on the bed and grabbed a pillow, smothering my face with it, screaming as loud as I could. After I finished my therapeutic shrieking, I sat up and opened up my laptop, feeling determined. I went to the "Jobs" tab on my LinkedIn page and decided I would apply for at least one position in the Greater New York City area.

My life had been stagnant for too long. For the following thirty minutes, I scrolled through page after page of boring job listings, updating and re-updating my search terms, before I found one that I deemed worth even clicking.

Closet Assistant: Condé Nast

Congratulations, Condé Nast—you had my interest. I secretly despised the idea of rearranging someone else's closet but I could harness those emotions for the greater good of a potential life achievement.
Desired Skills:
Bachelor's Degree √
Interest in fashion and Condé Nast publications √
Strong interpersonal skills √
Strong Microsoft office skills √

Could it *be*? Could I actually be *qualified* for a job? Maybe my mom was right. Maybe my life *would* turn around—and the past few months had been one of those downturns in life that I would joke about with my coworkers later. I checked the rest of the list.

Five to ten years of experience in online publications

I double checked the title of the job I was looking at to make sure I hadn't accidentally clicked on "CEO," or something important like that. Who, in their right mind, with 5-10 years of experience, would apply for a job to make $35,000, before taxes?

I slammed the computer shut, as there was nothing it could do for me. Lying back on the bed, I stared at the ceiling. That was the problem with peaceful reflection: your thoughts were your only company.

At what point do I have to realize my situation is not just a bump in the road? At what point do I simply accept that this is going to be my life? —that I'm not going to achieve greatness, that I'm just going to become another person who slaves away at a job I hate, settles for a bald guy with a beer gut and then dies without accomplishing anything of significance.

My inner peace was broken by the sound of my sister's voice bellowing through the house.

"Chelsea! We're ready for dinner!"

I rolled off the bed, as if I'd had the toughest day since Kennedy dealt with the Bay of Pigs incident, and I made my way toward the door, grabbing a sweater on the way out. There was nothing worse than getting to a restaurant that decided the arctic weather was ideal, meaning you couldn't enjoy your meal because you felt hypothermia setting in.

At some point, I would have to accept that life was just one big disappointment after disappointment, but it was dinnertime.

"Hey, Chelsea—how was your day?"

"Hey, Dad."

I don't know why I was always so morose when greeting my dad. It probably had to do with the fact that he was one of the most successful people I knew. He was so productive, day in and day out, while I spent most of my time eating and napping on the couch. I guess I felt a little bad that he worked so hard, while the only thing I worked hard at was painting my nails without getting nail polish all over my fingers.

Rachel, Sarah, my mom, Dad and I piled into my dad's car and headed for our favorite sushi restaurant, Sagi, which was the typical Japanese restaurant—wooden tables and chairs, a sushi bar across from the door, and those tan folding screens—with the Japanese characters on them—the ones that everyone secretly wanted in their room when they were younger.

As we followed the hostess, dressed in traditional Japanese garb, I saw someone who looked strikingly similar to my first boyfriend, Greg. He had short, dark brown hair, a medium build and face that looked oddly similar. There he was, sitting across from a bleach blonde who, from just the back of her head, I could tell it was his new girlfriend. I regretted not changing my outfit and doing my makeup. I thought about pretending I didn't recognize him, but considering we were in a restaurant that was smaller than most New York City apartments, I decided escape wasn't feasible. If I went up to him, at least it would have been on *my* terms—so he wouldn't come up to catch me stuffing an entire piece of sushi in my mouth.

My heart began to race as I walked toward him. He'd been my first boyfriend—my first everything—and for about six years of my life, we played the tennis game that typified 21st-century relationships, until he found a blonde girl who he believed was his soul mate. As with most ex-boyfriends, I imagined him dying alone, while I married a beautiful, successful manly man, so I think saying I was genuinely happy for him was a bit of a stretch.

"Well, this is really happening. I'll be right back."

"Where are you *going*?"

Rachel had asked a valid question, but I didn't have the time or energy to explain the intricate workings of my mind.

"I'll be right back."

So there I was, standing at the side of his table. I was pleased to see the look of shock on his face when he looked up at me.

"Hey—long time, no see."

"Hey, yeah, it's been a while. What's up?"

He seemed hesitant, like he was wishing I hadn't come over. What did he have *against* me? *I* was the one who wasted my best years on him!

"Oh, not much. Just having dinner with my family."

"Cool. Oh, uh Chelsea—this is my girlfriend, Jamie."

Jamie—what a terrible name! It reminded me of a middle school girl with frizzy red hair, freckles and glasses. It was unfortunate to be cursed with certain names, like Bertha or Mildred. Jamie was no better.

"Oh, hi—great to *meet* you."

That might have been the second most popular lie told in America. It wasn't *great* to meet her. I hated her hair, her voice, and I even hated her face. Yet I smiled politely.

"Yeah, you too."

"So what have you been *up* to?" Greg shrugged.

How *dare* he ask me that question? Didn't he know that my "Current Location" on Facebook hadn't changed and I hadn't updated the "Places I've Worked" field since my summer internship? Then I remembered I had "unfriended" him after he dumped me, after I got tired of seeing his stupid face every day on my newsfeed.

"Oh just doing a lot of sketching. I'm actually starting my own line, or trying to, anyway it's really exciting."

Two lies in the course of three minutes! I thought about submitting it to the Guinness Book of World Records.

"Yeah? What's it look like?"

My head whipped around and stared her right in the face. How dare this Jamie chick ask me anything! Didn't she *know* it was a two-person conversation, and she was just an intruding bystander?

"It's chic, affordable fashion for the 20-something girl."

"Oh, I have a friend who does that. She actually started it when she was 16."

"Yeah, well this is *different*. Anyways, it was great seeing you, enjoy dinner."

I shot her one of the nastiest glances I could come up with.

"Yeah, you too. Tell your family I said 'hi.'"

"Yeah, I will. I'm doing really great, by the way. Life is just really, really *great* right now."

Nothing said your life was going up in flames like telling someone about how great your life is going.

I walked back to the table and sat across from my mom.

"Oh, who was *that?*"

"Greg—that kid I dated in high school."

They all turned and looked. I'm not sure what part of answering a question about who I saw implied that they needed to look.

"Oh, *that* guy—talk about a *loser!*"

My dad always had such a great way with subtlety.

There was only one thing that was going to make me feel better. I opened the menu and prepared to order an excessive amount of food. Eating was one of my top ten favorite things about living at home. Parents were obligated by law to take their children out to eat with them, and since eating disorders ran so rampant in the United States, parents weren't allowed to tell their children—even the adult ones—to order less food.

"I think I'm gonna get the *niyumen* soup, a spider roll, a shrimp tempura roll, and I kinda want *gyoza*."

"Do you want to *split* the shrimp tempura roll?" Rachel asked.

Leave it to the skinny sister to ask the fat sister to split something! I always considered that someone asking you to split something *when you had intended to eat it all* was one of the top ten most awkward encounters. If she were someone else instead of family, I probably would have just sat in silence and stared at that thoughtless until mental telepathy took over and they knew I wanted to gorge without judgment. But it *was* family, and there were no rules with family.

"Uh, no. Not really."

"Really? Okay. Well maybe I'll just have one of yours, because I don't really want an entire roll."

"Okay... Well, I'm kind of really hungry, so *maybe.*"

I hadn't eaten lunch, and I was a growing girl! When the waitress came over, and I could feel her judging me as I recited my list of food desires.

"So how'd your *date* go last night?" Sarah asked.

I had forgotten that Sarah wasn't around when I recounted the horrors of the previous night. I really didn't want to have to go over it again.

"You went on a date last night?" Dad asked. "When? Didn't you have dinner with us?"

"No, Dad—I was not at dinner last night. I went to Firebirds for Happy Hour."

"Oh. Well, you missed some really great steaks. They were cooked to perfection."

Yeah? Well Dad—you missed some really great dinner entertainment!

"Wait! So how *was* your date?" Sarah pressed.

"It was terrible. He was a weirdo, and I'm never going on a date ever again!"

"Okay! Well I was just *asking.* You don't need to have such an attitude!"

"I've told this story so many times, and it was one date. I don't know why you guys care so much about my life!"

Rachel's laughing made things worse. Who was she to laugh at me just because I wanted them to stay out of my business?

"Chelsea—don't talk to your sister that way. She was just curious. Anyway, you always attract such *strange* people. I think it's probably because you're too approachable."

Thanks, Mom. Note to self: Be less approachable.

"Uh, yeah... I guess so."

Sure, Chris broke my heart, and I have had fewer boyfriend offers than Taylor Swift, but I could be queen to the weirdoes at least—a positive spin on my situation, I guess. I know my mom didn't mean to be rude, but I was having trouble seeing how "only attracting weird men" was a positive thing. That was the funny thing about compliments—most of the time they weren't very complimentary.

I devoured my soup in less than five minutes, grateful for the fact that stuffing my face kept me from having to answer any more questions about my personal life.

"So are you excited for the party tomorrow?" my mom asked, to lighten the mood.

Was I excited to attend a party celebrating my younger sister's bright future, while simultaneously celebrating my demise? No, Mother, I was not!

"Yeah, I think it'll be really fun."

It wasn't a complete and total lie. I thought the *money* part would be fun. I'd had some time on my hands, which I had dedicated to late-night infomercials. I had my eye on *The World's Best Blender*, and my graduation party funds would be enough to cover it.

I really didn't have funds for frivolous purchases, but I decided the blender was an investment in my future. I already had a toaster oven and electric tea pot, so I figured that if I bought enough essential appliances for a typical New York City apartment, a job wouldn't be too far behind. My belief was based on the whole "you can only get a date when you have a date" theory, except I had adapted it to "you can only get an apartment when you've already bought the appliances."

"We'll need *drinks*," Dad insisted. "Did you girls buy everything for the bartender already? We can't *not* have drinks. That's ridiculous."

My family had become major cocktail people over the last few years. I guess that was a perk of living at home, you had access to all the good alcohol your parents can afford that you never could.

"We're going to get them Friday morning," Rachel explained. "We already have a list."

It's amazing how we can be surrounded by so many healthy, fulfilling relationships, and yet we cling to the broken ones as if it were a life and death matter. We spend our lives desperately trying to get in, trying to connect with those who would rather throw us away rather than investing in relationships with the ones who value us.

In that moment, it seemed to me that human beings were emotional masochists. We thrived on being rejected, crawling after the affection of those who rejected us. I was one of them, and I couldn't find a way out.

After having cleared our appetizer plates, the waitress brought over our sushi and my order of *gyoza*. I had managed to snarf down two *gyozas* when I felt my phone vibrating from my purse. My parents' always had a rule about phones at the table, but after my dad discovered Facebook a few years earlier, that rule had become more of a guideline. I glanced at my purse and saw it was a 212 area code, which meant New York. I had to answer it.

"Excuse me. I need to take this. I'll be right back."

Before anyone could object or ask any questions that would delay me answering the phone, I rose and hurried out the restaurant.

"Hello?"

"Hi. Is this Chelsea Carlton?"

My heart was pounding. I could barely form the words to respond. My big moment had finally arrived!

"Yes, this is her."

There was a silent pause that seemed to last for ages, though it was probably just a few seconds.

"Hi Chelsea—I'm calling because you filled out an entry form to win a cruise, and you were selected as one of our *winners*!"

I paused.

"I'm sorry... *What*?"

"*You* won a trip for two to the Bahamas on a Carnival Cruise, and we just need a *bit* more information from you!"

My heart sank. The only thing worse than *not* getting a phone call from a prospective employer was getting a call from an unknown number, *thinking* it was a prospective employer. There really should have been a law, restricting soliciting calls to postgraduates. I thought about writing a bill and taking it to Congress. It might have been a bill that Congress could actually agree on.

"I cannot afford a free Carnival Cruise! I'm unemployed, you stupid idiot!"

I hung up the phone. It was at times like that when I longed for the days of flip phones. *An angry hang up was so much more passionate when you could slam something shut instead of angrily tapping your index finger on your touch screen.*

"Everything *okay?*"

I pursed my lips, closing my eyes tightly as I heard the familiar voice right behind me. I turned to see Greg and that ridiculously blonde girl, Jamie, standing there. How was it that, with 524,600 minutes in the day and infinite number of places people could be, we always seemed to run into the people we don't want to see, exactly when we don't want to see them?

No, everything is not okay! My life is in shambles and everyone, including you, has it figured out — except for me!

"Yup, it's great. Everything is just *fucking* perfect!"

I stormed past them on my way into the restaurant. I had wanted to seem so well put together that he would realize what he missed out on, that I had completely fallen apart. Well, not completely. I withheld my criticism on her bleached blonde hair, which would have put his perception on my mental health over the edge.

As I rejoined the table, I shoved my phone back into my teal purse and began shoveling more *gyoza* in my mouth.

"Who was that?"

Please don't make me explain it, Mom.

"Just one of those stupid free cruises you enter for at concerts. It was a New York area code, so I thought it might be a job, so I wanted to answer it. But it wasn't, obviously."

My sister, who had just taken a sip of water as I made the comment, began laughing, with the water in her mouth—as if I told the funniest joke of the century. *Nope, not a joke—just my life.*

"I'm sorry! It's just funny that it ended up being a *cruise*, because you don't really need a vacation, since you're on a semi-permanent vacation right *now*."

Two more sushi pieces went into my mouth.

"Sarah—don't pile on, but Chelsea—you *know* what I always say: don't expect too much and you won't be disappointed. If you had answered the phone not expecting a *job*, you would have been pleased with the cruise."

I had heard that saying more times than a Nun has heard Hail Marys, and it was one of those sayings like "sticks and stones may break my bones but words can never hurt me." You knew deep down it was true, but knowing the truth behind it never helped.

Seeing the dejection in my face, my mom reached over, consoling me.

"*Something* will come your way. You just need to wait."

"You're doing what you need to be doing," Dad added. "It's *fine.*"

Hearing my dad back up my mom's faith in me made my eyes water. I'm not sure why. Maybe I felt guilty that I wasn't fulfilling my potential, or it was the self-loathing that was threatening to become part of my psyche. Either way, I spent the rest of dinner fighting back tears.

I texted Bridget after we got in the car. She was all over the place, doing field work for her masters, but I knew she was home for the weekend and would want to go out.

8:00 pm: Let's go out tonight! Pint's?

Bridget 8:05 pm: Yeah. Wanna come over?

8:06 pm: I'm on my way home from dinner. My parents can drop me off.

"Can you guys drop me off at Bridget's? We're gonna go to Pint's, I think."

My dad's voice was barely audible over the music.

"Really? I don't know how you guys can go there, it's so bad."

"Yeah, well I don't really have a ton of options, so that's where were going."

We had talked as a family all through dinner and the entire car ride home, but as the conversations wore on, I couldn't help feeling the weight of an intimate realization crushing me. As I sat there, listening to them I suddenly felt like I didn't fit in here anymore. I felt different. It was as if I was an outsider, watching the scenes of the movie play out, and something was out of place—me. I'd become a stranger in my own life.

My home was supposed to be my salvation, my safety net but it felt more like a prison now. At school I was free. Now, it was like I was being told who I was supposed to be and what I was supposed to feel. Still, I was worried that if I didn't fit in L.A. and I didn't fit there, did I fit anywhere?

Chapter 8

Pint's

I hurried up Bridget's driveway and twisted the knob on the side door of her house, which they always kept unlocked. It was perfect, because I always hated the awkward, "I'm at the door and no one is coming to let me in," situation.

I found Bridget sitting in her kitchen sipping on a Pimm's cup. She had studied abroad in London(while I was in Paris), and she had gotten both of us addicted to them. We couldn't afford the ingredients on our own, but her parents sometimes had a nice stock that we were allowed to tap into.

I found a second drink sitting on the table across from her, waiting for me. She knew me too well. I took a gulp before recounting my night for her.

"Guess who I saw at Sagi tonight?"

"Who?"

"Greg... and that *girl* he dates now."

"Are you serious? She's so gross, but wait—that's so awkward. I wish I was there."

"It was so bad. I had to go up and talk to them, and I played it *so* cool. Then I got a call that I thought was a job offer, which turned out to be one of those cruises you enter for at concerts. I screamed into the phone—*how I couldn't afford a free cruise?*—and guess what? When I turned around, and there he *was*."

When she laughed, I couldn't help but joining her, realizing I had come to the right place. Between chuckles, she managed to respond.

"No, he *wasn't*! Did you *say* anything?"

"Yup. He had the nerve to ask me if everything was okay, and I said 'it's fucking perfect—probably better than *your* life."

Whenever we retold stories to each other, we always left a 10-50% margin for embellishment.

"At least you got some good sushi out of it. If it makes you feel better, I had to change an 85-year-old man's diaper today."

We both laughed. That was the thing about old friends—it was never necessary to talk things through and offer condolences. *Laughter helped, along with a few Pimm's cups.*

An hour later, we were up two friends and down an entire bottle of Pimm's. Kenzie and Ashley showed up after I had got there, and we were busy making plans for the night and discussing our futures, or lack thereof.

"Okay, so the guys are going to Pint's now, and James said he could pick us up. Do we wanna go?"

Kenzie had always been our key communicator with "the guys." When I say "the guys," I'm talking about the same boys we'd grown up with—the ones that we'd gone through our awkward stages with, the ones we had some of our best times with and the ones who were there when we suffered through the unbelievably sad times.

Some might think the shared experiences would have made us a extremely tight knit group, a *Breakfast Club* kind of group, but we weren't—at least not in the superficial sense. We had a strong bond because we'd been through so much together, but when it came to us versus other girls, we usually lost out. Yet we went back to them, time after time, like bees to honey.

"Ugh! Do we have to hang out with the guys? I don't *want* to."

Bridget complained every time we decided that we were going to hang out with "the guys," but she ended up having the most fun in the end. The battle of us convincing her to go had become a part of the nightly routine, like putting on makeup or eating dinner.

"Bridget, come on—if we *don't* go, we're going to sit in all night, and we haven't gone out in so long!"

Ashley had a point. Our lives had become a lot of "wine nights" and very few "leave the house nights." The point of social functions was to brag to other people about how great your life was going and make them feel bad about theirs. When you are unemployed social functions became a lot less desirable since the only exciting thing to report was that you finished every season of *Grey's Anatomy* in two days.

After five minutes of convincing her that we needed to leave the house, and that the outing would be big fun, we were headed out the door to James' car.

We piled into the car, just as we had for the past eight years. If I thought about it for too long, I started to worry that we'd still be doing the same thing in another eight years. I noticed one subtle difference as we made our way down the list of regular questions that consumed our conversations.

"How's school going?" was missing from the lineup.

It no longer made sense to ask, since none of us were still in school, so the only plausible answer would be, "not at all," but I still felt a strange sense of nostalgia well up within. Never again would I be asked that question, which I had been asked for sixteen years. It's not that I wanted to go back to college, but there still was a strange sense of anxiety knowing that, with one strut across a stage, that chapter of my life was over, just like that.

It always amazed me how quickly things ended, and how, once they were over—something that was your entire life—how that once important something could feel like nothing more than a faint star, twinkling in the distance. I was living in California less than a month earlier, but it felt like a lifetime away. Nostalgia was a side effect of changing perspectives, or maybe it was just a side effect of too much alcohol.

Ten minutes later, we pulled into the Pint's parking lot. We climbed the wooden stairs leading up to the back porch and walked in through the side door. There were two different doors at Pint's. First, there was the main door, which led to the restaurant part of the bar. By restaurant, I meant a room that looked like the product of a one-night stand between a bar and a diner. The wood booths served as a nice border, with a small bar in the middle.

There was a second entrance on the side deck that led to the outside bar. It provided a more casual setting where no one would complain if someone else was wearing flannel pajama pants or some other unusual getup. It was like being on the set of *Cheer's*—except the low budget version.

Since my town had a population that was less than the number of celebrities who had joined Scientology, I recognized a group of people across the bar, sitting around a table against the back wall. They were some of my high school comrades. We had played sports together and had intersecting social circles, but my desire to be around any of them had faded, like my dreams of any employer who would take pity on me.

"I'm going to the bar. What do you want?" I quickly asked.

"Gin and tonic."

"Vodka cranberry."

"Vodka water."

It seemed the three of them already knew I was going to ask, which made me imagine how great life would be if *all* of our decisions were so easy. *What job do you want?* Entry-level, making from 30,000-40,000 but in an industry that interested me. Where is your relationship going? We'll move in together in about 6-8 months. All the questions we spent hours, days and even months obsessing over would have been easily solved if we applied the "What do you want to drink" theory. It was a matter of making a decision, and if it wasn't the right one, *you could make a different one.*

I climbed up to the bar, and two minutes later, the bartender appeared. It might have been a shanty bar, but I'd never gotten faster service anywhere else.

"A gin and tonic, Vodka cranberry, vodka water and a Jameson and ginger."

I didn't really care for Jameson. I always felt a little bit like I was swallowing fire when I drank that Irish whisky, but it somehow made me feel like I didn't *really* belong back home. It played into the fantasy I'd been living—that I was actually living in New York, working at a great job and just visiting for the weekend. The only problem with fictional fantasies was facing the truth, when there was no great job, and I wasn't visiting for the weekend. I was stuck in a small town, surrounded by people I thought I had long since left behind.

I took a big gulp of my Jameson and ginger, fire and all. I was staring at my glass, lost in thought, when the bartender returned me from my fantasy world.

"You do know we don't have a *limit* on the amount of times you can come up to the bar, right?"

He was cute—definitely older than me, and I was sure I'd seen him there before. He had dark brown hair that left me wondering if it was a hairstyle or if he hadn't been able to find his comb that day. His t-shirt had a vintage look to it—or maybe he couldn't afford laundry, because he was working at a bar at age 25 or older. Whatever it was, the shirt clung just enough to his body to outline his muscles. For a moment, I thought it was part of my fantasy world, but after careful consideration of my surroundings, I decided he was the real deal.

"Yeah well, it was either get the first round of drinks, or spend extra time, pretending to be interested in people who you barely wanted to pretend to be interested in, in high school."

I glanced over at Kenzie, Ashley and Bridget. They'd found a table near our "friends" from high school and sat down. Seeing that the coast was clear, I headed over. For once, I was glad I had to carry four drinks across a bar, because it gave me an excuse to do the casual "Hey how are you?" without having to stop and actually listen to anything someone had to say. As I grabbed the drinks and was walking away, I heard a voice behind me.

"It's not so bad if you just give it a chance. You'll see."

"Yeah? You'd think 22 years would be enough of a chance." I turned ever so slightly, partly because I was trying to be coy and partly because I had four drinks in my hand. Any sudden movement would cause me to drop them—$16 plus tip, down the drain.

"Hey, guys..." I said, turning to the four girls at the table next to ours.

As much as I wanted to keep going, I couldn't walk by without saying anything.

"Hey what's going on?"

"Nothing, really. I'm apparently a *waitress* now, though," I sighed, nodding toward the four drinks I was carrying. My signature laugh signaled I was being sarcastic.

"Here's your vodka water, Ashley..."

We all started laughing, as the comments piled on. Ashley claimed she drank vodka water because she liked the taste, but we knew the truth—she didn't want to afford the extra calories that a mixer added.

That was the worst part about people who were trying to be skinny—they also tended to be full blown liars. For a society so obsessed with being thin and looking good, people were quick to lie about what they did to be thin. It seemed the entire world wanted to be thin and desirable, but no one wanted to *admit* they wanted to be thin. It was strange.

We'd only been at the bar for half hour before I saw a group of kids walk in. By kids, I mean they were 24-ish, and we'd all gone to high school together. Since they were two years older than us, we crossed paths a few times here or there, at one party or another, and I'd *dated* one of them—Scott.

By dated, I mean it in the most modern sense of the word. We texted now and then, over the years, and we had gone to get ice cream or saw a movie once or twice, but our "dating" consisted mostly of hooking up. He was in no way ever, my boyfriend. Most of the time, we never admitted to anyone that we hung out, or at least *I* hadn't.

We'd started talking again occasionally during the last few weeks of my senior year, after a guy I met on spring break broke it off with me and I needed someone to take my mind off him.

It was the first time I'd seen him since I'd been home. I'd officially seen more of my romantic interests in the last 24 hours than I had

in the last two years. It was going to be a long
year of living at home if the pattern continued.
*Why couldn't my parents have stayed in New
York City instead of settling down in such a small
town?*

When the four guys walked toward our table,
I went to the default awkward encounter
position and pretended I hadn't seen them.

"Hey, haven't seen *you* guys in a while. Hey,
Chelsea!"

I turned from my seat at the end of the table
so that I was half-facing him. He looked thinner
than the last time I saw him. Maybe post-grad
life would grant *me* the same blessings. Eh,
based on the way *my* life was going, I'd probably
be the first person to *gain* weight while living in
poverty.

"Hey Scott. How's it going?"

"Pretty good. Didn't expect to see you here."

"Yeah, me either." I shook my head.

"Okay, well I'm gonna go get a drink."

Good conversation. In actuality, it was one of
the lengthiest face-to-face conversations we'd
had in almost a year. Better take it slow. After
two more rounds of drinks, my friends and I
engaged in all the necessary social graces, and I,
like everyone else, was feeling rather...drunk. I
was enjoying myself, until one of our "guy
friends," Joe, walked into the bar.

He was average height, with short brown
hair, and his baggy jeans perfectly matched his
Oakley t-shirt to form the trifecta of the "I'm too
hot to care" look. For years, I'd racked my brain
trying to figure out why girls found him

attractive, because I could not, for the life of me, figure it out.

His nose was strangely shaped and he had less interesting tidbits to share than Paris Hilton. Things just came naturally easy to him, which earned my spite. Kenzie started dating him in high school after a difficult chase. Their relationship ended about as well as The Lewinsky Scandal when she found out he'd been cheating on her the entire time. But that was four years earlier, and he'd been chasing her ever since. She had a habit of giving in, which drove me nuts. It was a power chase for those two— they only wanted each other when they couldn't have each other.

I saw him coming towards us, so I made a bee line to the bar. I wasn't drunk enough to deal with him yet.

"Hey, Chelsea—"

"Pleasure as always, Joe."

It was hard to blow off his innocent hello, because ever since we'd graduated from college he'd worked so hard at being a normal human being and not his usual, douchebag self. But the new Joe was more creepy than nice. Maybe I could see through his act, or maybe he'd been his old self for so long that it was too late to change.

I planted myself at the bar across the room and sat there, drinking alone. I didn't mind, though. Sometimes when I spent too much time around the people I grew up with I actually started to have fun, and that was something I wouldn't let myself do. I was afraid if I let myself have fun, I'd get used to being here and I'd settle for never leaving.

Kenzie met me at the bar fifteen minutes later.

"Joe is so ridiculous that it's insane. He keeps saying how he *loves* me and wants to be with me. He won't leave me alone!"

I knew that Joe had been texting her since she came home for the summer—not to mention the years before, but I never knew what to say. Kenzie didn't do much to discourage him, although any attempt would have probably been in vain.

"Yeah but don't you still text him? So doesn't that kind of, you know, give him *hope*?"

"What am I supposed to do, Chelsea?—not respond after he's texted me 15 times in a row? We're in the same friends group, so we're going to *see* each other, but it's not like I want to *be* with him!"

"Oh well, I don't know."

"And he's still hanging out with Jenna! She's such a slut! I hate her, so if he wanted to be back with me, he shouldn't hangout with her. Why is she even here?"

I hadn't noticed that she had walked in until Kenzie informed me.

Personally, I didn't think Jenna was such a slut for hooking up with someone's boyfriend. Knowing Joe, I highly doubted he did much protesting when Jenna was throwing herself at him. In fact, I don't even think Joe and Kenzie were together when he hooked up with Jenna—at least not in his mind.

I didn't think it was the girl's fault. Naturally, Kenzie didn't agree and repeatedly warned me that "you will never understand until it happens to you," to which I had to agree. True, I didn't know what it was like, but that didn't stop me from forming my own opinion..

I always thought that part of the reason Kenzie couldn't find a job was because she already had a full time position as a Jenna Hater. As females, we hold onto anger, but it doesn't mean that anger controls our lives. Most of the time, it lied dormant, simmering, until the time came to use it. We all had a Jenna, but there was something about the situation that just got under my skin.

"I don't know, probably because it's one of the only bars nearby."

It seemed logical to me.

"Well, she should *leave!*"

At that point, Bridget had come over and was standing next to Kenzie. I'd never been more grateful to see her in my life.

"Guys, I just did three pickle back shots! They're so good! We need to get some."

"Look! Joe is talking to *Jenna.* I can't *believe* it. She's so disgusting! Why is she even here?"

She just wouldn't drop it!

"Kenzie! Why do you care? If you don't want to be with him why does it even matter?"

"Because she's gross and I don't want to be around her!"

At that point Bridget had chimed in.

"I mean, she's gotten *better.*"

"No, Bridget, she's gross! Are you serious?"

I could feel the anger boiling inside me. I was a volcano, about to burst.

"Yes, she's serious. This is so *stupid*! It's so stupid I can't even believe we're talking about it still. No offense, but I don't want to spend my night talking about you and *Joe...* and how unattractive *Jenna* is."

I tried to flavor my words with slight sarcasm, but they sounded condescending and rude and tasted like acid as they came out of my mouth. I wanted to take them back, but I couldn't. I realized I had gone too far.

"Uhm, okay... Why are you being such a *bitch*?"

"Because this is all *bullshit!* I mean, come on! Am I the *only* one who notices that we've been talking about the same thing for four years? Not to mention the two years before that—when we spent all our time talking about how much of an asshole Joe was! Before you even started dating! It's all *bullshit!*"

At least they were listening.

"Honestly—if I never heard about you and Joe and you're insignificant fucking problems again, it would be too soon! You act like he's the worst person in the world, and Jenna is a terrible person, but guess *what?* She doesn't owe you *anything*, and you give *into* him, so you're fucking *asking* for it! It's bullshit, and I'm over it."

It was official. I had snapped. It was bound to happen, considering I'd been building up that energy ever since summer, when Chris broke my heart into a thousand pieces. While I was picking up what was left of my heart off the ground,

Kenzie had a guy who was dying for her attention, so part of me was jealous. The combination of the frustration of my life, jealousy of hers and the Jameson in my glass, I had reached my breaking point.

"Really? *That's* how you're going to treat me, after all the times I've been there for you?" Kenzie complained.

"Like when?"

"Uh, maybe like today, when you were crying in your car, and I was there for you?"

"Wait," Ashley broke in. "*When* were you crying in your car? What did I miss?"

I ignored her, continuing the showdown.

"That's very different than you forcing us to listen to your drama for the last 100 years—about one of literally the worst guys I've ever met."

"Uh, so my *Dad's* here?" Bridget said, in a valiant effort to diffuse the situation, but it was too late.

"I'm fucking *out* of here!" Kenzie fumed.

I expected a harsher response, but I think she was just shocked. I looked toward Bridget, searching her face for a sign, confirming that she understood where I was coming from and that I wasn't out of line. Then she gave me a hug.

"I guess I could have handled that differently," I admitted.

"I mean, I think the message was right," Bridget sighed, "but the *delivery* could have used some work."

We both laughed.

"Want a ride?"

"No, I think I'm gonna stay a little. Thanks, though."

She waited a moment, allowing a little time to reconsider my decision.

"Okay. Well, text me when you get home."

"Yeah, I will."

Telling someone you'd text them when you got home after a night of drinking was one of the most commonly broken promises among twenty-somethings. It was like New Year's Resolutions—despite good intentions, in the end, few followed through.

By then, the bar had cleared around me as I sat alone on a barstool, grabbing my phone from my purse. The blinking red light shined at me from the background. I was prepared to open another spam email when I pressed the unlock button, and saw a new text message.

Chris: 1:35 am: See you tomorrow.

It was Chris. I hadn't communicated with him for a full 24 hours since our last message, when I confessed that I wanted to see him too. In turmoil of my day, I had actually forgot about it. What game was he playing? He texted me and told me he missed me, but then he didn't mind that we went hours without talking? It didn't make any sense, just like everything else in my life.

1:40 am: Yeja

By "yeja," I meant yea. Incoherent text messages were also a side effect of drinking. I had been looking down at my phone when I heard a voice and felt someone sit down next to me.

When I looked over and saw Scott, I noticed how much more muscular he was than the last time I saw him. His face, though, looked exactly the same. He was wearing athletic shorts, sneakers and a t-shirt. It was like a scene from *Cheers*, but instead of wanting to go *where everybody knows your name*, the cast at Pint's wanted to go *where you can look like you're going to the gym*.

I glanced at my drink, just sitting there staring until he broke the silence. This whole night was becoming too much.

"*That* looked rough. What's *wrong*?"

"What's wrong? What's *wrong*? My *life* is in shambles, and I don't even know how to change it!"

My voice cracked as I rushed the words out. I could feel the tears welling up in my eyes and I wanted to cry, but I strained to keep my emotions in check. However, my mouth did not get the memo.

"Oh you mean specifically what's wrong?" I took a sip of my drink. "Let's see here. I'm not qualified for any job, besides volunteer work. I have no money, no love life and the guy who broke my heart into a thousand pieces has a radar on me that tells him when I'm finally doing better so he can screw up my head!"

I could feel Scott staring at me, and I could feel my face getting hot and red. I knew the tears were inevitable.

"Yeah well, I know how you feel. I'm two years out, and I can't find anyone to hire me. I'm coaching 7th graders in Soccer... for free."

"I know. I get it. It takes time blah, blah, blah. But I'm not supposed to fucking *be* here! I'm supposed to be successful, and my life was supposed to fall into place. I did everything *right*. I'm not supposed to be sitting at this fucking Podunk bar, with all of these people who are stuck in high school bullshit. I was always supposed to be the one who really made a name for herself—the one who had great stories to tell people about how great my life was. I don't know what to *do* anymore!"

I noticed he glanced down at his beer. In all the years I had known him, he was never one to discuss his emotions. He always ran whenever he felt emotionally attached. I may not be a romance expert, but even I knew emotional heart-to-hearts was not a turn-on for most guys at bars.

"I *know*. It's bullshit!"

He said four words—four simple words, but that was it. When I felt the first tear fall and hit my hand, I saw him glance back at the rest of our high school comrades. They were laughing and having fun—maybe being perpetually stuck in high school worked for some people, but not for me.

He took a swig of his beer and I followed suit, finishing the rest of my fourth drink. As I put the glass down, he looked at me so hard I could feel it. I assumed he was trying to figure out how to appropriately escape, leaving the crying girl alone at the bar. He'd never been a bad guy—even during the times we weren't on good terms I never thought of him as a bad guy.

"You wanna get out of here?"

I nodded.

He finished off the rest of his beer in one big gulp, and we headed toward his car. When I got in the passenger side of his grey Ford Explorer, I realized it was the same car he had in high school, when he would take me home from parties or dates. The entire night left me feeling like I was in a time warp. The windows were down and the hot, humid summer air brushed across my face as we drove to my house. I stared out the window into the darkness at the familiar roads and landmarks, thinking, "Is this really *all* there is for me?"

"It's gonna be fine, you know? I know that's what you're *supposed* to say to everyone, but for you—it really will be. We may have had a rough past, and I know probably said a lot of shitty things to you, but you're gonna do something great. It may take time, but you'll get there. I can feel it. I always could."

Turning from the darkness, I looked up at him. I didn't know what to say. I didn't even know if the things he said made me feel better or worse.

"Yeah, well I'll be sure to give you a shout out during my *E! True Hollywood Story.*"

I felt him smiling as he laughed before pulling up to the front of my house and putting the car in park. My heart raced. I never did well with uncertainty—whether it was with my future career or the simple uncertainty about if the guy who gave you a ride home and saved you from embarrassment at the town bar was going to kiss me.

We sat there, both staring forward, staring at nothing—staring at anything *except* each other.

"Thanks for the ride."

"Thanks for the ride," was the go-to saying in high school when you were getting dropped off by a guy and *wanted* him to kiss you. It was outdated and I hadn't used it in four years, but I figured that when it came to time warps, if you couldn't beat em, then em.

He leaned over the center console, turned my face towards his and kissed me. I let him. I wasn't sure if it was the alcohol, my loneliness or true emotions, but I felt the butterflies start to flutter in my stomach.

With our lips still touching, I smiled and gave him another quick kiss before turning toward the door.

"You know, at twenty-four, I've gotten my parents to extend my curfew till *morning*."

It was clever, I definitely gave him an A for effort, but I knew what would happen if he came inside. It wasn't that my parents would mind—they knew Scott, and I think they'd be relieved to know that I wasn't A-sexual. I knew that if he came inside, we'd end up sleeping together, and we would wake up the next day, freak out and not talk the rest of the summer. My heart was still racing, I wanted him, but I had to resist more.

"Lucky you, but I've got an early morning. I'll see ya around."

I closed the car door behind me and rushed up the driveway, though with every step, I thought about turning around and inviting him in. I just reached the garage door when I saw the taillights of his car. I guess *he* was hoping I'd change my mind too.

I stumbled to my room and grabbed a t-shirt out of the bottom drawer of my dresser, and I had just managed to slip into my bed as I heard my phone bing. Fumbling over the keys, I opened the text message.

> Kenzie: 2:05 am: I know Joe is bullshit. I know all this old drama is bullshit. I fucking hate that I'm still here wrapped up in it, but right now I have nothing else, and I'm sorry. I just wish I could find someone else I liked as much as I liked him and could forget all about him.

Kenzie had never been one to extend the first olive branch, so I had to reread the text a few times before believing I actually received it.

> 2:06 am: Yeah, me too. Sorry, I overreacted. Love you.

> Kenzie: 2:07 am: Love you too. See you tomorrow.

I felt my phone slip from my hand and fall to the floor with a thud. Thirty seconds later, I was asleep.

Chapter 9

The Final Hours

"Chris, what are you doing? You should go. I can't do this again."

"Chels, time-out—I'm here because I love you, and I know you love me too."

"No, you don't. You just like the *idea* of me, like the idea of us all hanging out—you, me, Matt and Rachel—but I can't be your second option. I wish I could, but I can't."

"You were always my *first.*"

As his lips met mine, I couldn't resist kissing him back, my hands exploring his back, feeling the usual rise and fall of his muscles. He was strong, but not overbearing. My hands loved every inch of him. I could feel him pulling me towards him, my body letting him. The space between us closed...

"*Waakee up!* It's *party* time!"

I heard the familiar voice and felt the familiar shaking of someone trying to wake me from sleep. As my eyes popped open, I grabbed my pillow, holding it as tight as I could against my chest. My heart pounded through my chest as I struggled to breathe.

"Whoa! What's going *on* with you?"

Rachel's voice was barely audible over the sounds in my throbbing head.

"Nothing... I'm fine. What are you doing?"

"Really? You seem jumpy."

"It was just a dream. I'm fine."

"A *good* dream?"

Her eyes scrutinized my face and eyes, searching my soul the way only a sister could.

"No, a *nightmare* actually."

I hadn't completely lied. It *had* been a nightmare to me—having to confront Chris and discuss our feelings was something I dreamed about all the time, but I'd never stayed asleep long enough to know the outcome of the conversation, and it *terrified* me.

I lied back on the pillow, trying to slow my breathing.

"Rachel, I need to sleep more. Go away."

I was normally an early riser, and I really didn't mind being forced out of bed early—even if I had only been able to get a measly *seven* hours of sleep. It was more the principle that bothered me. I may have been living at home, but I wanted to retain a measure of control. Choosing when and how to wake up was pretty much the last semblance of autonomy I had in life.

"I'll leave, but seriously—you need to wake up, because it's already nine o'clock, and we have a lot to do before the party."

Once I heard my bedroom door close, I rolled over and reached for my phone, which had fallen to the floor. With one eye open, I saw ten new emails—all spam of course, and no new texts. As I checked my phone every morning, I never expected any messages of grandeur would be waiting there, but I always hoped for a pleasant surprise.

I made my way to the bathroom, where after five minutes and a strong burning sensation in my eyes, the mirror revealed my fresh face. Since

I was gonna have to do makeup again later for the party, I wanted to give my face a little bit of a break. I wasn't sure how much we had to get done during the day, but I hoped it wasn't a lot of outside errands. The likelihood of someone seeing me looking like a pre-rehab meth addict was lower if I didn't leave the house.

"Good morning, Chelsea. It's *party* day!"

Even my mom had jumped on the party brigade bandwagon, but such cheerfulness from everyone so early in the morning was only making my hangover worse. I staggered my way over to the Keurig and popped a K-cup in before even acknowledging anyone. It was too early and I was too hung over for this

I wondered if it was too late to cancel the whole event. Then I saw my younger sister and realized we *couldn't* cancel the party. She had so much to celebrate and so much good ahead in life. She deserved to have her accomplishments acknowledged, even if I couldn't acknowledge mine.

I pushed my hair out of my face with my hands, as if wiping the hairs off my forehead would take away the tension pushing against my eyes. My mother's face finally came into focus.

"Yeah, do you need help with anything?"

I kept repeating one phrase, over and over in my mind: *Why did I drink so much? Why?*

In truth, I wasn't really capable of helping with anything at that point. I needed some serious breakfast before I could even think about doing any real work, but offering to help felt like the polite thing to do at the time. It was kind of like asking how someone was—no one really wanted the honest answer—most often they asked just so they didn't look like total assholes.

"Well, the food's pretty much done, but we need to set up the tables outside, get ice in the coolers and decorate the tables."

Awesome. Nothing helps a hangover like physical labor.

I felt my Dad's voice vibrate through my body.

"Don't forget about music! We need *music!*"

"I'll just put some CDs in, because we can't hook an iPod up to the sound system." Rachel said.

"*Sure* you can," he disagreed.

"Okay. How?"

"I don't know, Rachel, but there's gotta be a way. Just figure it out. *You* guys are good with technology, find some app."

My Dad was notorious for the term "there's gotta be a way." He was a fairly tech savvy person, but he definitely overestimated the powers of technology. He assumed that, because you could jam all your music into one device and because you could transfer money on your phone, there had to be an app to do everything. It was a great, proactive attitude, until there *wasn't* a magical app, and I realized I wasn't smart enough to develop one for his every wish and command.

"I'm gonna go with Rachel to get alcohol. Where's Sarah?"

If I was going to be forced to share a graduation party with an 18-year-old girl, whose future was already brighter than mine, I was going to make sure she pulled her own weight in this whole "set-up" thing.

"She's at Tara's house. I told her she had to be home before noon. So don't worry—she's going to do her part in setting up for the party."

Tara lived down the street and had been my younger sister's best friend since we moved into the neighborhood when Sarah was five. The only similarity they had was their age, considering she was a foot taller than my sister, and her clumsy, lanky body always kind of reminded me of a puppy learning to walk for the first time.

"Are you ready to go?"

Rachel was wasting no time.

"Yeah, let's go. Uh, actually, hold on. I just have to run to the bathroom really quick."

After finding myself huddled over the toilet, I made sure to wipe my face and make sure there were no signs of the lingering effects of a night of binge emotional drinking. Returning to the kitchen, I grabbed my satchel, shoved my phone into it and threw it across my body. I grabbed a Pop Tart from the kitchen, because I could feel the hangover walls closing in, and if I threw up in my sister's car, I'd feel a wrath worse than Hell.

The thought about going to a store that sold liquor made my stomach churn as we drove. I rolled down the window to get some fresh air and threw a piece of Pop Tart in my mouth to calm my stomach. I wasn't sure if it was the alcohol from last night or the anxiety about tonight but I felt sick.

I felt her staring at me even before she opened her mouth. It's funny how you can hold a curling iron against your finger for a long time before you begin to feel any pain, but you can feel someone staring at you the second they turn their head.

The only thing more awkward than knowing someone is staring at you is letting them know you know they are starting at you. I fought hard to keep my head turned toward the outside of the window, wishing my heart would stop beating so loud—I was afraid she could hear it. I knew what was coming, but I tried to pretend it wasn't.

"So... Chris is coming."

There it was, the elephant that had made its way into every room my sister and I occupied since September—all squeezed into her small sedan. I always thought that beginning a heavy and uncomfortable discussion during a car ride gave an unfair advantage to the attacker. It was like guerilla warfare for social conversations, and I couldn't get away—even though the thought of jumping out of a moving vehicle seemed more appealing than facing a conversation about my unrequited love.

"Yeah, I uh, I heard."

"Well, have you guys *talked* since..."

She paused, unsure about how to continue. I finished her question.

"Since he dumped my heart into the *gutter*?"

I had two options: I could tell the truth, or I could lie. If I told the truth, I would be forced to surrender my pride and admit that, although I pretended I enjoyed being single, my secret wish at 11:11 every day was that he would make some grand gesture, and we'd spend our lives together. Or I could lie, but I guessed she already knew the answer to the question. She was dating his brother, and I doubt she would have brought it up if she thought we hadn't talked since.

"I guess a little. I mean, he texted me a few times. We *barely* talk."

"Are you excited to see him?"

The truth was, I didn't know *what* I felt. I was excited to see him, because I hoped he would confess his undying love for me, and it would be like none of the bad stuff happened. We would just go back to how we were last summer— carefree and casual.

I knew my fantasy was definitely not going to happen, I mean this was Jersey not Hollywood and I wasn't the star of some romantic comedy. The night was already doomed and I'd probably spend next week binge eating greasy Chinese food and watching Netflix. My only real concern now was if my mom would feel bad enough to foot the bill for my Chinese addiction.

"I don't know, I guess."

"You *guess*? What does that even *mean*?"

"What do I *mean*? I mean he fucking broke my heart into a million pieces. I was dead, and I haven't felt the same since, so forgive me if I'm not jumping for joy that after eleven months of him treating my heart like a doormat, he wants to see me."

I had intended for my rant to come out with more of a sarcastic tone, but I projected my anger and frustration with Chris on her instead. Even the thought of him made my hairs stand on edge. The craziest parts of me came out, and I had projected it on her.

"Okay... sorry."

I sensed the hurt in her voice. Rachel had never been particularly sensitive, but when it came to Chris, something about her changed, and it was one of the few times in life I felt we had the bond that sisters were supposed to have.

I returned my gaze to the window while she returned her gaze to the road ahead, neither of us saying anything. As we pulled into the parking lot, I knew I had to break the silence before we stayed silent so long that it would become too awkward to break it.

"I know you're sorry, and I know you didn't mean it like that, but he makes me so crazy— even the mention of his name or knowing that he's even still alive. I can't get out of my own head when it comes to him, and I *hate* it! It's so hard, because I love him and I want to marry him and have his babies. But then at the same time, I kinda wish he'd get hit by a bus."

The inner conflict that people who were passionately in love and passionately rejected experienced can be compared to the severity of conflict a vegetarian has when they're starving, but the only thing being served is meat. It was awful, and I had been experiencing it on a daily basis for almost a year.

"Well, maybe he won't come."

"Yeah... maybe."

I don't know why I said it, because I didn't mean it at all. I had bought $8 fake eyelashes, which increased my getting ready time by 20 minutes, because I'd inevitably end up gluing my eye shut and would have to redo my eye makeup at least twice.

I'll probably be more upset if Chris *doesn't* show than if he shows and breaks my heart again. Or at least I think so. Generation Y guys were nothing more than "movies based on books." You took a chance, hoping it'd be great, but in the end, it always disappointed, which meant girls dating them had become conditioned to downsize their hopes, which were never really that high in the first place.

We grabbed a cart and made our way for the liquor section. I was looking down at my phone, catching up on all the horribly uninteresting things my friends had posted on various social media platforms, when I heard someone call my name.

"Hey Chelsea."

I looked up and saw one of my guy friends standing there. That morning, I had gone with the messy bun and *au naturel* lack of makeup look, which I very rarely did for this exact reason. It's not that I ever had feelings for him or cared that much about what he thought of me, but my plan was for everyone to see me looking flawless at the party so they'd forget I didn't have a job... or a boyfriend... or any sort of future.

"Hey, Tory. You're coming tonight, right?"

"Yeah, I get off work at six and then I'm heading over. Can't wait."

"Great. See you then."

Short, sweet, to the point, and maybe he didn't get a good glimpse at the giant pimple that is forming on my forehead. While I was talking to Tory, my sister finished off the last few things and was already at the register.

"Can I see your ID, please?"

My sister fumbled with her wallet and handed the woman working behind the cash register her license.

I was playing with my phone when I felt the clerk staring at me. I glanced up just long enough for her to squeeze in a quick demand.

"I need *yours*, too."

"I'm not *buying* anything. She is."

"It's our policy to ID everyone who is in the store."

I knew what this was about: if I had piled on some makeup and was about five inches taller, she wouldn't have even asked to see my ID. But because I looked like a child bride, I had to prove I was old enough to buy liquor. It was like going through airport security every time I wanted to exercise my right to buy liquid therapy! I heard the voice of someone definitely under 21, and when I looked behind me, I saw a girl who was probably eight years old, at the check-out counter with her dad.

"Are you going to ID *her*?"

The cashier looked at me like I had just asked her to ID a dog.

"Who?"

The sarcastic undertone in her voice only made my blood boil.

"That girl over there with her Dad."

"No, we don't ID children."

"I thought you ID'd everyone."

"Not children."

"You never know. He *could* be buying her alcohol, and you know what alcohol can do to children at a young age, right?"

"What?" she muttered as she rolled her eyes.

"It can stunt their growth and then they'll end up like me, facing discrimination while just trying to purchase a little bit of beer."

People had been standing up against discrimination for years, and my moment was no exception. I thought I had really gotten through to her.

"I need your ID."

Maybe not. I grabbed my license out of my wallet and handed it over. No one said standing up against discrimination was easy.

She packed up our goods and we headed out of the store.

"It really is ridiculous that just because we're small and look young that *we* get ID'd, and no one else does."

Rachel, even smaller than me, shared in my annoyance.

"Yeah, I mean I never considered myself a martyr, but based on my performance back there, I think I might have a career in it...How much do *martyrs* make?"

"I don't think the make anything..."

Well, that did it. I couldn't afford to be a martyr, at least not yet.

I felt my phone buzzing in my pocket, and when I looked at the name on the screen, I immediately pressed the ignore button.

Why was Chris calling me? Didn't he know I couldn't handle phone-to-phone conversation? I know talking on the phone increased communication effectiveness, but I wasn't prepared to give instant responses to whatever he wanted to know. That was the glory of texting—I could be the best possible version of myself because I had time to decide the best way to respond. If there was the same lag time in real life, then my relationships would have gone much better.

It still felt strange though, ignoring his phone call. Last summer, we talked all the time, and I wouldn't have felt the least bit nervous at picking up his call. But my stomach tied itself in knots and I felt uneasy when I saw his name. It was like when your parents called, after they sent you a "we need to talk" text.

How could my attitude and disposition toward him change so much in one year? Instead of having a casual conversation with an old friend, I was sitting in my sister's car, having a private panic attack.

When I heard my phone go off, I expected it to be Chris, but what I saw was even worse.

Scott: 12:30 pm: Hope your morning wasn't too rough. There's no way you'll be able to answer all the questions about your post-grad plans hungover.

Scott texting me precisely at the time when Chris called me was the exact proof I needed to solidify my most logical standing theory. The only thing you needed to get a guy to like you was *another* guy to like you. The main problem with my theory was the *choosing* part, and I usually chose wrong.

12:32 pm: Yeah, it was rough, but I think I'll make it.

Scott: 12:34 pm: That's good. I have to coach a lacrosse tournament, but I'll be over around 9 or 10 probably.

He'd be over around 9 or 10? Why was he coming over? I didn't invite him to the party... or did I...

All of a sudden I had a flashback from the night before—when we were sitting in his car, and I not only let it slip about the party, but I told him he should come. For that specific reason, I made sure I was 100% sober when I invited all of my friends on Facebook.

The bigger problem with drunk Chelsea giving out invitations was that presently, I had *two* love interests coming, when I barely had the emotional capacity to handle one. That meant I would probably end up losing them both, and I would wake up the next day with an absurd amount of sent "please forgive me, I love you" texts.

One theory I was planning on testing was the "If you delete someone's text, did they even text you?" notion. True to my socially awkward form, I deleted his text and decided the best course of action was the no-response course.

I could hear Jimmy Buffet blasting from the kitchen speakers even before we opened the garage door.

"Wasted away again in Margaritaville..."

We'd barely reached the kitchen, but I could already hear my dad singing, even louder than the speakers. Rachel nudged me in the arm as we walked into the kitchen.

"I guess this officially kicks off the graduation party."

In between Jimmy Buffet serenades my dad gave out cooking orders, like a general, instructing his troops before going into battle.

"Put the alcohol in the front hall, and then Chelsea—I need you to start cutting more cheese for the mac-n-cheese, and then Rachel—you can help Sarah make the barbeque sauce."

I looked around the kitchen as we manned our battle stations. Jimmy Buffet's voice filled my ears while a sight I hadn't seen in a while filled my vision. There we were, all of us, in one place—and there weren't any boyfriends or friends—it was just us as a family working together.

In that moment I learned an important life lesson. My life would be full of changes. Sometimes I'd be up, and sometimes I'd be down, but I'd never have to face anything alone, because we, as a family, were together in that war called "Life."

I felt more secure than I had at any other time. Maybe my mom was right—maybe we would be all right. I didn't know what the future held, but in that moment, it felt like everything would work out. That was the true power of family.

"So the cheese is done, and I'd love to stay and help, but unfortunately, I need to go get ready, because it's already 3:30."

"Chelsea—that's an hour and a half. You do not *need* that long. You look fine."

It was the single biggest lie mothers told their daughters, "You don't need all that makeup. You look fine the way you are." *Then one day, you decide to trust her and leave the house without makeup. Everywhere you go, people ask you if you're sick.*

"First off, Mom, you *have* to say that because you're my mom, and telling your child they need makeup is punishable by DYFUS, so I'm gonna go get ready."

"I'm so glad I grew up when I did, because we were so natural, and I couldn't put all that makeup on all the time."

She had been making the same point to me for years— telling me how I didn't need so much makeup and then reminding me about how much easier life was back in the day. As if I didn't know that already! I mean, I'd much rather have been at Woodstock, living off the land and some hallucinogenic drugs, than on LinkedIn every day, begging for a janitorial job.

My little sister chimed in.

"Yeah, remember that time you looked like Ugly Betty."

"Yeah, Sarah, that was great and considering I was woken up at three am because the alarm went off and I had my retainer in and glasses on. I'm not *even* going to get offended by that comment."

I heard the laughter coming from the kitchen as I made my way up the stairs. Looking in my bathroom mirror, I realized I'd be lucky if I could be ready in an hour and a half.

As I lined my eyes, I started to wish I was a guy. They had it so easy! All they had to do was hop in the shower, wash what minimal amount of hair they had, throw on a collared shirt and some jeans, and they were ready to go.

Unlike me, who had an hour and a half process ahead, and that was only if I didn't take breaks to change the music. I was really starting to feel down on the whole being a female thing when it hit me: "Women and children first." It made me feel a little bit better.

When I heard the doorbell, I knew it was time to put down my weapons of mass makeup and accept that it was as good as it was going to get. Hopefully at least one of my two prospects would like what I came up with.

My coral dress was just long enough to hit the floor. Besides adding four inches my heels made me seem much longer and skinnier than I actually was. The dress crisscrossed in the back, revealing just enough of my tan skin that I didn't give off the "this is a formal, pinkies out party" vibe, but I still looked classy enough so that my family wouldn't regret giving me money. I took a deep breath before heading downstairs.

Chapter 10

One Last Round before the Knockout

By the time I reached the foyer I saw that most of my family had arrived—a pretty good turnout, which was great, because they'd probably be the main donors to the "Chelsea Carlton Post-Grad Foundation." I had just finished making the rounds when I saw Kenzie, Ashley and Bridget walk in the front door.

I breathed a sigh of relief when I saw them. I was worried they wouldn't be the first of my friends to arrive, meaning I'd be forced to mingle outside of my immediate social circle. Most people moved to a new place after college and found a job, surrounding themselves with people they *didn't* know and were forced to mingle and make new friends.

On the other hand, I was stuck at home, where I didn't have to socialize with anyone outside my family, and on the off-chance I did, I mingled with the same people I had known since kindergarten. A side effect of being an unemployed post-grad was the inability to socialize outside comfort zones.

"Let's get a drink!"

I corralled my friends, herding them toward the bar. I had no idea if or when Chris was going to show up, but if I was going to make it through the night, I would need some liquid courage.

"Only if we're doing *tequila* shots!"

"We are definitely *not* doing tequila shots. This is a grown-up party."

"We got dropped off tonight *by our parents.* This is definitely *not* a grown-up party."

The last time I had a party and Bridget forced me to drink tequila with her, we both ended up running down the street and sleeping on the front lawn of one of our elderly neighbors. It wasn't until we were woken up by EMTs that we even noticed we'd fallen asleep. It turns out the 80-year-old woman who lived there thought we *died* on her lawn.

Fortunately, we were let off with a request to go home and not let it happen again. Drunken antics were funny when you're going into college, but once you've graduated it just became depressing. Perception had a way of ruining even the most fun situations.

Kenzie held up a glass.

"Let's toast."

"What do *we* have to toast about?" Bridget asked.

"Jobs?" Ashley proposed.

"Nope," we all responded in unison.

"Boyfriends?" Kenzie suggested.

"Nope."

We were all single.

"Better days?" I blurted it out without thinking, but it worked.

"To *better* days!"

We toasted to better days, we toasted to old memories, we toasted to friendship, we toasted to all the guys who didn't *want* us, we toasted to the jobs that denied us and we toasted to toasting. Before I knew it, I was drunk, and it was barely seven o'clock.

I felt Kenzie's hand grab my arm before I even heard what she said.

"Is that Chris?"

Turning, I saw the panic on her face and realized I hadn't told any of my friends that he was coming. Maybe I was embarrassed, or maybe I didn't want to admit that I missed him, but most of all—I think I wanted an excuse to talk shit about him with them if he ignored me all night.

"How dare he show up to my party uninvited and ignore me?" had more merit than, "I waited for him, I invited him, he *still* doesn't want me."

"What? Oh? I don't know. Where?" Deny, deny, deny.

I glanced around the room, straining to see where she was pointing. By that time, a group had gathered by the bar, and I was too short to see over most of them, even with the extra four inches.

I spotted him, coming down the hallway with Matt. They looked enough alike that you'd they were related, but Chris was shorter and had a more lean build than Matt's. Part of me—no, *most* of me had hoped he'd gained weight or gotten a weird haircut since I last saw him, but he hadn't. He was exactly how I pictured him in my mind, and in my heart.

His hair swept away from his face. I could see his chest and arms, outlined in his dark grey cotton t-shirt. I used to hate those tan cargo shorts—they made me feel like we were going to the river to fish, but they didn't look so bad now.

I took another sip of my drink and headed toward him, my heart was beating so fast that I could feel it pounding in my brain. I hoped *he* couldn't hear it.

Mr. Alterman stepped in front of me.

"Chelsea!   Hey—congratulations   on graduation!"

Like most love-stories, there were obstacles. Mr. Alterman was above average height, with a receding hairline. He had graduated from Yale and had a decent amount of success as a restaurant entrepreneur. He therefore thought he was smarter than everyone else and thought we all needed to know it. He'd been friends with my parents for years so I'd gotten used to the condescending comments.

"Hey, thanks for coming," I smiled, extending my hand.

I tried to look past him to see if Chris was still standing there.

"You   graduated   with   a   *Fashion   Design* degree, right?"

"Yeah."

"Taking the easy way out, I see, but who can blame you when you're at such a fun school in California."

"I minored in Business Management, and I graduated with a 4.0."

"I bet *that* was tough. So what are your plans *now*?" he said, grinning.

I stared at his face. He was smiling that arrogant smile that said, "I bet you wish you were like *me*, don't you?" His   tone   was condescending,   but   there   was   something different about me, though it was a situation that resembled other recent encounters. It might have been that I was sick of answering the question, but it was more likely the four gin and tonics I had flowing through my bloodstream.

"Nothing. No one will hire me, so I'm doing fucking *nothing*! Please excuse me."

Pushing by him, I hurried down the hallway. I felt my face getting hot, I knew I needed some fresh air.

"Hey!"

I felt Chris's hand grab my arm as I raced past. It felt like fire and ice and made me stop in my tracks.

"I need to go!"

Ripping my arm from his grasp, I raced toward the back door. A few minutes later, I sat at the side of the house on the grass next to the electric meter. It was the best place I could think to hide.

"What *happened* back there? I know you hate me, but there's no way all that anger came from seeing my face for twenty seconds."

I didn't want to laugh. I didn't want him to know that he still had me, but I couldn't help it because he did—he still *had* me, *all* of me.

"I'm just tired of explaining myself to people. I'm tired of feeling like my life is standing still, while everyone else is moving forward. I'm tired of not knowing if I'm ever going to do anything remotely significant in my life!"

He took a long sip of beer before responding.

"I don't know how you pull me in every time."

I didn't know what that meant. I didn't know if I *wanted* to know what it meant. We sat there, both of us, just staring at our drinks, as if *they* were going to tell us what to say or do. It was silent, but I'd never heard anything so loud.

"Well, I don't know, *either*. I need to go."

I hoisted myself up and made it three full steps before I heard his voice.

"I don't *know* what it is. I've tried to let it go, and honestly, sometimes I think I have. But then I'll watch a TV show or listen to a song, and I realize how different last summer was from this one, and *you're* the only thing that's changed. Seeing you tonight and you being mad at me right now makes me realize how much I miss you. It kills me, because seeing your face when you saw me—I saw how much I hurt you and I wish I could change things. Sometimes, I even wish I could change my feelings for you, because it would all be so much easier, but I can't change the past, and I can't change how I feel now. "

I was scared to turn around. I was scared that if I looked at him, I wouldn't be able to walk away and I'd end up alone and heart-broken again. That was the thing about having a broken heart—you spend hours, days, months and even years wishing the person who broke it would come back to you and heal your heart. But like most broken things, even if you repair them, they just aren't the same.

I turned around anyway.

"Well, my drink's all gone, so I should probably go, but I'll see you around."

"I'll see you later."

I stared at him for a moment before heading back inside. I looked back one more time just to make sure that he hadn't been a figment of my drunken imagination. It wasn't. Part of me wished he had asked me to stay—wished he made me tell him I felt the way he did. But he didn't, and I wasn't surprised. It was not the movie scene I imagined. It was real life.

"Were you just outside with Chris?" Bridget accused.

"I'm sorry. Did I *miss* something?" Ashley cut in.

"Why is he here?"

Two steps into the kitchen and they found me, the three voices of reason I couldn't ignore.

"Yeah, but nothing happened. We were just talking."

I don't know why I didn't tell them what happened. It was probably because a big part of me still believed he would change his mind. And telling my friends how Chris finally confessed his feelings for me and then having to tell them that, in the course of a few hours and a few beers, he had changed his mind—that was something I was not prepared to do. So I omitted a few details about our interaction.

Kenzie knew I'd been lying.

"Wait! *Really?*"

"Yeah, let's go get a drink."

There we were, back at the bar—just the four of us. Sure, some of our other friends had come in and out, and were mostly gathered outside, but we were all we really needed. In the midst of the chaos of our changing lives, it was nice to know one thing was constant. We had each other, and that was all we needed. We toasted to Chris, we toasted to me, we toasted to old memories, we toasted to mac-n-cheese and we toasted until we felt like our toasts were going to come back up.

By the time we had finished our toasting, the sun had gone down and most of the parents had left. As we stood in the kitchen, we could hear music and the mumbled voices of forty twenty-somethings, coming from the basement—all of whom were just as lost and confused as we were.

Ashley was drunk, but her logic seemed intact.

"So are we gonna go *down* there?"

"Do we *have* to? We should just stay up *here*."

"Bridget, we need to go down."

"Yeah, we probably should go down. We've been ignoring everyone all night."

I slid open the basement door, and as we walked down the stairs, we were transported into a low budget *Great Gatsby* film. The main difference was that, instead of fancy champagne flowing, we were drinking from red solo cups, filled with vodka that came out of a plastic bottle and cost less than the dress I wore.

Despite our lower class version, we were all there. We might have been lost in our lives and didn't know where we were going, but we were together–right where we belonged.

"Hey I haven't seen you all night. You look nice though."

"Hey Drew I know it's been crazy, thanks for coming. Where's your new girlfriend?"

"She ended up going home for the weekend. Probably better anyways."

By that point, the alcohol had flowed through everyone just long enough that they had started playing charades. As you get older and the world starts to change around you—you cling to anything you can that resembles the older days. Even if that means playing childhood games while drinking copious amounts of alcohol.

"So have you talked to him?"

I was still staring at our friends when he broke the silence.

"Who?"

Yeah that's smart, just play it cool.

"You *know* who. Chris. I know this is hard to believe but I know you, so I know there is no way he has been in your presence for an entire night without some conversation happening."

"I mean, we talked. I don't know. I don't really wanna talk about it."

"Yeah I get that but you're too good for him. He doesn't deserve you."

He pulled me in for a hug as the last few words slipped out of his mouth.

"Thanks..."

My voice was hesitant. I tried so hard to believe him but I also had once seen all the good things in Chris and wasn't ready to accept that we weren't good for each other.

"I just want you to know that I feel really bad that we kinda lost touch, and the real reason the girl I'm dating, well was dating, didn't come was..."

"Hi I love you I'm leaving though."

Kenzie slurring her words had interrupted whatever Drew wanted to say and I was too drunk to remember we were even having a conversation.

An hour later, just about everyone had left. Those of us who remained sat in the kitchen, picking at the leftover food. They were mostly my sister's and Matt's friends, who lived too far away to drive home that night. Eating drunk is a lot like exercising—it starts *off* well, but then it takes a turn for the worst at some point, and you realize what a terrible mistake you made. I hit that point with the mac-n-cheese and I decided it was time to call the party officially over.

"Well, everyone—it's been real, but I'm going to bed."

I hopped down from the counter, glancing over at Chris, searching for a sign to convince me he didn't regret what he said earlier. I saw nothing. Feeling frustrated, I just let it out. I thought it was a whisper, but in a state of advanced intoxication, nothing was ever a whisper.

"Fucking *awesome!*"

I walked toward the stairs slower than I ever had—giving him a chance to follow me. When I realized he hadn't moved, I felt my heart sink lower into my stomach.

Grabbing an oversized t-shirt from my floor, I tripped into my bed and wriggled under the sheets. Through my drunken stupor, somehow I managed to realize that Scott never showed up. I thought I would have two guys fighting for my attention that night. Instead, I was in bed alone, feeling sick from the piles of mac-n-cheese I just ate.

That was the problem with expectations— things are never is as good as you think they will be. I felt a watershed of tears surging, but my mind shut off, and I was asleep before the first tear could fall.

Chapter 11

The Morning After

My head was spinning and my eyes felt like there was a weight pushing against them from the inside. I could already hear people talking downstairs, and the voices only made my headache worse. I'd been smart enough to pull my blinds down before I got in bed, so I wasn't forced to face the day, yet just enough light managed to get in so that I was forced to face myself.

Something wasn't right. When I looked down, realized I wasn't wearing the same shirt I wore to bed, and it didn't look like any shirt I'd ever seen before. I tried hard to remember what happened, but it was like looking at my reflection in a foggy mirror—I got a vague idea about what happened, but the details weren't there.

I felt the weight of a body next to me, and glancing over, I saw it—one of the biggest mistakes I could have made. It was Chris, sleeping peacefully in my bed. I watched his bare chest rise and fall for a few seconds before it all came flooding back to me.

I was already asleep by the time he came into my room, but I woke up when I felt him crawl into the bed. I remembered having a conversation, but the details of what was actually said were vague. We could have discussed anything from getting married to buffalo chicken dip.

I knew I needed to wake him up and face whatever this morning was going to bring, but I didn't know how. Before our bend-up, I would have just rolled on top of him and forced him to get up with me, but everything felt so fragile—like one wrong move would bring the entire earth crashing down on me again. As experiences with people change, so does our perspective about them. I tried shifting my body in bed—just enough to shake him awake without making me have to actually do it.

"What are you *doing*?"

He pulled me back down and held me close to his chest. My heart wanted to forget about the past and stay right where I was, but my head wouldn't let me.

"I can't do this. I want to, but I can't. I'm sorry."

"Chelsea, stop."

"Actually, you know what? I'm *not* sorry. I'm not sorry at all—not even a little. I'm *more* sorry about the two pieces of cake I ate last night than I am about this. So how's *that* feel?"

I didn't want to admit that I ate two pieces of cake, but when you have to make a point, you have to make a point. Plus, he almost definitely saw me naked last night, and I wanted him to know, if we were to ever do it again, I would be a little skinnier. I waited for him to tell me how wrong I was. I waited for him to tell me anything. All I heard was laughter.

"What? Why are you laughing? Is there something *funny* about me still being emotionally attached to you? You're *unbelievable*! *Honestly*?"

I sprung out of bed and grabbed some sweatpants off the floor. I couldn't believe it was actually happening again.

"I'm calling a timeout on your mental breakdown, because I need to tell you something that might help you along."

"What? What could you *possibly* have to tell me that I don't already know? I *know* you just want to be friends. I *know* I'm a super awesome girl, and you *love* hanging out, but you just don't like me like that. I know *all* of that! Why did you even come up here? What do you *get* out of it? It's *sick*, really!"

I'd been so busy ranting that I didn't notice my pacing put me within his arms reach. He grabbed me around the waist and pulled me close, his touch sending chills down my spine.

"Honestly, there isn't anything I can tell you that you don't already know. I think I love you. You *knew* it—even when I didn't, even when I pushed you away. I came up here last night because, for the last nine months, all I've thought about is going to bed with you at night and waking up with you in the morning. You're right. You *are* an amazing girl, and I do love hanging out, and I do want to be friends with you, but I don't want to be *just* friends."

I felt my heart start to race and tears welling in my eyes.

"I can't pretend that everything in the past didn't happen."

One of the biggest self-sabotage techniques involved getting everything you wanted, but insisting on that extra bit of reassurance—so you push the person one step farther away. It was my typical move. I was inclined to insist that someone *prove* they loved me in order to convince me of it. The technique had a rate of 0% success to date.

"I'm not asking you to pretend that the past didn't *happen*. I'm just asking you to *believe* that we have a future."

I kissed him and he kissed me back, there were no words left. I had planned for so long what I would do and what I would say if he ever came back to me, but in the end, I had two choices: I could play it safe, or I could take the risk, put myself out there and accept that I may be loved in return.

We stayed in bed for another hour, maybe even longer. We would have to get up sooner or later and face the world, but I wasn't ready to— not yet.

Unfortunately, my family was.

Rachel: 11:52 am: Come downstairs. We have bagels.

11:54 am: Where's Mom and Dad?

Rachel: 11:54 am: They went to the farmer's market.
You and Chris are safe.

It was times like these that I was glad to have sisters. Brothers wouldn't have thought like that, but sisterly intuition was good to have for these types of situations.

I made sure to change my shirt before heading downstairs. There was no telling when my parents would come home, and as lovely as having a hung-over discussion about *whose* shirt it was sounded, I wasn't in the mood. Living at home was like being in a police interrogation room, except you didn't get breaks for good behavior, and there was no such thing as the 5th amendment, because the wardens were paying for your meals.

The boys had this thing about eating their breakfast at the wooden table outside our basement door, it was some strange ritual, but it gave me time to catch Rachel and Sarah up on the events of the night before. Sarah had a way of prying into my personal life, but she did it in such a genuinely inquisitive way that I couldn't hold it against her.

"I'm not *saying* anything, but can you explain to me what's going on?"

"I don't know. I fell asleep, and this morning I woke up, and there he was."

"And... I mean, are you *okay*?"

Rachel, unlike me, held out high hopes that Chris still had feelings for me and the problems of our past were the result of him being scared about how *much* he cared for me. I think she also liked how close we had become last summer and was hoping it would be that way again.

"Yeah, I'm fine. I think. I mean he told me he *loved* me."

We sat there, staring at each other for what seemed to be forever.

"Well, at least *someone* does, because I don't know if you've seen your hair this morning, but you look like Bellatrix LeStrange from *Harry Potter*."

True to younger sibling nature, Sarah was able to break the awkward silence with an insult.

The boys came back upstairs a few minutes later to say their goodbyes.

For a while, I thought he wasn't going to say goodbye to me. I didn't need a grand, romantic goodbye, but a simple "Adios Amigo" would have been nice. Then I heard his voice from the front door.

"See ya later."

And then he was gone.

I felt nothing. I thought I would be prying my fingers away from my cell phone to prevent myself from texting him, but I didn't feel tempted at all. I didn't know if this was what it felt like when you felt secure in a relationship, when there was no game playing, or if it was one of those moments where you finally got what you wanted, just to find out that the reason you wanted it was because you couldn't *have* it.

As I sat there thinking, I realized that neither option was good. On the one hand, I had been conditioned to think that security in a relationship was achieved when someone you've been chasing decided to give up on the idea of finding anyone else but you. On the other hand, I might have only wanted Chris because I couldn't have him, and if what I felt with him *wasn't* love, was I capable of *feeling* love? Like I said—neither option was very good.

Sarah rescued me from my thoughts.

"Okay, so for graduation tomorrow, I think we should go out for dinner *after* instead of before, since it starts at 3:00 pm."

Sarah's high school graduation was set to take place the next day, and as excited as I was for her, public outings were not joyous occasions for me, since the only accomplishment I had to talk about in my life was making it through another season of *Sex And The City.*

"Do I *have* to go?"

Chapter 12

Three's a Crowd

By the time I woke up from my daylong nap, evening had come. I grabbed my laptop from the counter, a beer from the fridge and headed outside to do some thinking in the hot summer air.

About an hour later Sarah joined me.

"What's up?" She asked as she sat on the lawn chair next to me.

"Beer?" I lifted a bottle in her direction.

"No, I'm okay." I set it back down on the ground.

"So what's it like being home?"

"Seriously?" I took a sip of my beer, "It sucks. I mean living at home isn't that bad, but it's the not making any progress towards anything I don't like."

"Yeah but at least you're working on sketches and stuff, when you have enough you can send them to stores and stuff right?"

"I can but it's not like they're going to pick them up. Honestly I don't even know if it's what I want to do anymore." I opened another beer, letting the cap fall to the ground.

"What do you mean? You've wanted to be a designer forever?"

"I always pictured myself as a designer but I don't know. After all the rejections I'm not sure anymore." Tears started to form behind my eyes, I tried to blink them away.

"You'll get somewhere. You're really good at a lot of things."

"Exactly! I'm good at a lot of things but I'm not great at anything." I sniffled and flicked the top of my nose with my hand. "I just always thought I'd have a certain kind of life, that it would just happen for me somehow and everyday it's more and more clear that it isn't going to happen. It's just hard to let go of it." I bit my lip.

"It'll happen, seriously. Just don't give up."

"Thanks. Sometimes you just have to you know? When the world is telling you that this path isn't for you, sometimes you should listen."

"Yeah, sometimes. But not this time. Do whatever you want but I think you should keep trying."

I just nodded and stared out into the darkness. I didn't know what I wanted to do. I felt broken but at the same time something inside me was telling me I was on the brink of a breakthrough. It was an unsettling feeling and I hoped it would go away soon.

My phone started to ring a few minutes later, reaching down I picked it up.

"Hey what's up?"

The voice on the other end surprised me. It was just before midnight, and I had assumed he was already out with the other guys or back in Philly.

"Are you home?"

"Yeah... I'm in the backyard. Why?"

"Okay."

Then he hung up. A minute later, I saw a shadow coming around the corner of my house.

"Drew?"

"Yeah, hey. What are you doing out here?"

He was panting as he spoke, like he'd just run a marathon.

"I'm," I paused, I wasn't sure what I was doing. "I'm sitting... what are you doing at my house?"

It wasn't some sort of made-for-TV teen drama series. My friends didn't just show up to discuss something—we *texted.*

"Well, Chelsea, here's the thing about life... do you have another beer?"

"Yeah... sure, here."

I grabbed him a beer from my secondary stash, meant for inspired writing. As I handed it to him, I could tell something was off—like he was drunk without ever drinking.

"So what's up? I thought you'd be out drinking or back in Philly by now"

"Yeah I was supposed to, but yeah, I'm not. Oh and me and Sam broke up."

"Sam? Who's Sam?"

"That girl I was dating. The one from Philly."

"Oh, uh sorry?"

I was still processing what he said by the time he asked for another beer. They broke up? I needed to know why.

Was it because of me? No, don't be ridiculous! It wasn't because of me. Plus, I had just slept with Chris—less than 24 hours earlier. Why did I even care? *I knew why I cared. I just wasn't ready for him to know why I cared.*

"Oh, yeah? Why's that?"

I tried to make the awkward pause seem much less awkward by taking a long sip of my beer—as if he wouldn't notice how long I'd been silent if I took a sip—like he actually thought this whole time I'd been thinking about the most efficient way to drink my beer. We both knew why I'd been silent.

"It just wasn't working. Family stuff, work stuff, you know—the usual."

Maybe we both hadn't known why I'd been silent.

"Plus I just didn't have a connection with her really. I mean sure having someone around was great and she's really cool, the guys love her but it's just not working."

Or maybe we had.

"Oh, sorry to hear that. There are plenty more fish in the sea."

I don't know why I said that, I always hated when people fed me that line. As if knowing there were other people in this world that were available to date eased the pain of not being with someone you loved! It was like telling someone who's sick about all the other diseases out there and expecting them to feel better about their lives. *I know you have cancer, but don't worry— AIDS hasn't been cured yet, so perk up!*

"Yeah…"

When he sat next to me on the lawn chair, I could feel my heart racing and my throat tightening. *Was it time to be concerned about having a severe allergic reaction to all this male attention?*

"I'll probably end up with *you* anyway, so it's not a big deal."

I know he meant it as a compliment, but it sounded more like an insult. *But I guess winning by default was better than not winning at all.*

"Yeah? Why's that?"

"Because you're my best friend—and a guy and a girl can only stay best friends for so long until something happens."

"Well, we've made it this long, so I think we're good."

We sat there in silence, listening to the familiar sounds of a summer night. His eyes were focused on me, and mine were focused on my beer bottle. I couldn't bring myself to look at him, because I knew if I did he would kiss me, and I didn't know if I was ready for that.

I tried to tell myself it was because I didn't want to ruin the friendship, but I knew better. Once one "best friend" developed feelings, it was just a matter of time before the entire friendship went up in smoke. I had been single for so long that I wasn't sure if I knew how to make the transition from being a "me," to being a "we." I had a choice to make—both of which had decisions that meant I'd leave the other one in my past forever.

"Chelsea, I just want to say..."

I looked up from my trance and was waiting for whatever was going to come next, but the iconic ring of his iPhone interrupted him.

"Hello? I'm at Chelsea's. What's up? Oh, you *are*? Okay, I'm coming."

"Who was that?"

"James. He's here, we're all going to Pint's if you wanna come."

"Oh... no, I'm good. Thanks, though."

"You sure? It'll be fun."

I couldn't help but laugh.

"I bet it *will*, but I'm okay. I should probably just stay home."

When we got up, I decided to go in for the friendly side hug to avoid any opportunity for him to kiss me, but he put both arms around me and forced me into a full frontal hug. My face was smushed into his chest and my nose was pressed so close that my breathing was restricted. Then he kissed my forehead. I pulled away before I could even think about what had just happened.

I was halfway through the door when I realized I needed to say something.

"Have fun tonight."

"Yeah, I'll try."

I smiled at him before stepping inside and shutting the door.

"What was *that* about?"

My sisters were sitting on the couch in our kitchen, watching *The Real Housewives* while feasting on a jar of Nutella. I hadn't even noticed them until Sarah said something.

Another problem with living at home: No privacy. Your every move was watched like you were the President of The United States, but without the added perks of private planes and a house with a bowling alley. I hated how my entire family commented on my every move. It made me feel like I was suffocating in my own life, but still, I grabbed a spoon from the drawer and sat with them.

"Nothing. Drew just came over for a little, and then the guys went to Pint's."

"*You* didn't want to go?"

I didn't know why Rachel seemed so surprised. Pint's wasn't exactly an exciting place, and she *barely* went out.

"Not in the least."

"Yeah, I mean I can imagine the bars would be fun, but *nothing* trumps Nutella and the kitchen couch!"

Sarah wasn't even 18 yet, so she was content that we didn't want to go to the bars all the time.

We sat there for a while, watching TV, all crammed onto one couch. We didn't have much to talk about, considering we lived almost every moment of our lives together, but it wasn't a silence that brought tension—it was the kind of silence that came when you were so comfortable around others that words weren't required to let them know you were present in the moment. The episode had ended by the time I spoke.

"Are you excited for school? You leave in like a month…"

"Yeah, I'm excited…"

The hesitation in her voice was strange. Anytime someone brought up going to college or the great state of Virginia, she acted like she'd just been given an overdose of happy pills.

"But…?" Rachel probed.

"I don't know. I'm really excited to go to school, and I love that I chose UVA, but at the same time I can't imagine not coming home and going to bed in my room every night. And the whole family is going to be going out to dinner or whatever, with me not *being* there."

Ah, an age-old problem about going out into the world and blazing your own path, discovering who you are—the people you leave behind. Even though you know it's the right thing to do and it'll be a great time, when you leave a place that's filled with people you love you get a strange feeling.

It's a rare form of guilt where you feel you're abandoning them. I remembered the exact same feeling before I left for California. I had even looked up the application deadlines for schools in Philadelphia, although I never went as far as applying.

I turned to the only wisdom I possessed to get me through that type of emotional turmoil. I told her what my mom had told me before I left

"I felt the same way, but it'll be fine. And just remember that it's our job to *miss* you, but it's *your* job to go and have a great time."

"Yeah," Rachel added, "and once you get there, you'll be so busy that you won't even have *time* to miss us."

"Well, darling sisters," I concluded, "it's been a pleasure, but I'm going to bed."

True to introvert form, I fled when things got emotional.

Minutes later, I found myself lying in bed staring at the TV as grown women bickered over what had to be some horribly insignificant issue. A quick beep, and blinking red light coming from my iPhone rescued me.

Chris: 1: 42 am: What are you doing?

Well, it was about *time*! I wasn't going to text him back right away. I wanted to make him sweat it out—make him really wonder if last night meant anything to *me*.

I tried to focus my attention on the mindless reality TV show that was playing, and after what had to have been an hour, I looked at my phone.

Really? It was 1:45 am? Only three minutes had passed? I couldn't resist the temptation of responding, so I decided that three minutes was enough time for him to significantly wonder where I stood.

1:45 am: Just lying in bed, watching TV

I waited by the phone, staring—waiting for him to respond. It'd been twenty minutes without a response, and by this time Bravo had traded the drama-filled lives of middle-aged women for the boring, yet ever-so-tempting, infomercials. With nothing left to occupy my time, I shut off the TV and went to bed.

I'd been asleep for half an hour before I heard my phone ringing from where I'd left it on the nightstand. I rolled over, and when I saw Drew's name, I pressed the ignore button. Drunk dials are like tequila shots—they can be very entertaining, but it takes a certain mental state to put up with them.

Drew: 2:50 am: Come outside.

He was outside my house? I seriously considered ignoring him, but I decided that if I was ever going to have a chance at a relationship that didn't consist of the other person convincing me I imagined it, I'd have to start now. Plus, I had no idea what he was going to say.

I pulled the retainer from my mouth, gave my teeth a quick brush and threw my hair into a bun. Fortunately, I'd chosen to sleep in my silk black and white polka dot shorts and tank top— and not the ones with the wiener dogs all over them. Everyone made fun of me for sleeping in matching pajamas every night, but I knew it would come in handy one day.

I was still partially asleep when I made it outside the front door, and saw him standing on the front porch, looking much less intoxicated than I thought he would be.

"What are you *doing* here?"

"I'm going back to Philly today."

"Okay...and what does *that* have to do with being at my house at 3 am?

I was getting angry. The only thing I disliked *more* than being woken from sleep was "guys who toyed with other peoples' emotions."

"I guess I just wanted to apologize, because I know you've always kind of thought that I bailed on our friendship, and I just want you to know that isn't true."

I didn't kind of think that, I *did* think that. After freshmen year of college, he barely spoke to me. *I never told him, but it hurt, a lot.*

"Okay, Well, good to know. Goodnight."

"It was just too hard with school and friends and stuff."

"What are you talking about?"

"You've always meant a lot to me and it was too hard to be here and you being across the country it was easier to end our friendship than manage my life here and be into you."

I suddenly felt the same way I had earlier in the night—except instead of feeling hopeful that I was loved, I felt discouraged that I never would be.

"Yeah, well I guess *that* didn't work out so well for you."

I felt bad. I knew I crossed the line. After a while I couldn't endure him staring at me any longer, so I said the only thing I knew would get me out of there.

"I'm going to bed. Have a safe trip back."

As I turned to go back inside, my eyes began to water. Earlier, when I felt I could never lose him, I didn't feel one bit emotional. But there, realizing I could never have him, I felt so much. I felt his hand grab my arm, as the first tear rolled down my cheek. The only thing worse than the disappointment of an unrequited love— was being comforted afterwards.

I was facing him, but I couldn't bring myself to look at him. I didn't even know if I felt that way about him still or if I was just lonely, but either way, I didn't like the way his rejection made me feel.

The next thing I knew, his hands were holding my face and I felt his lips meet mine. It was the kind of kiss that made me feel excited, confused, happy and scared all at once. It was the best kind there was. He pulled away from my face, his eyes fixed on mine.

"I should have chosen you from the beginning, but I'm choosing you now—only you."

It was like a movie scene. The romantic part of me wanted to stay outside with him all night, because I was worried that if I turned and went inside, I'd wake up in the morning and realize I'd dreamed the whole thing. But the realist part was telling me I needed to turn and run, because he was drunk, and in the morning he would realize what he said.

Dating in the 21st century taught women to assume there was an excuse before accepting that they were wanted, without exception.

"You may be one of the last good ones left. I'll see you around."

I squeezed his hand once more before heading inside. I'd gotten more attention in the past few days than I had in a while and now the only emotion I could feel was confused.

My room faced the front yard, so from the comfort of my own bed I was able to see him outside my window, still standing there in the darkness. It was ten minutes before I saw a car's headlights pull and take him away.

I lied back down and returned to staring at the blank TV. Within minutes, I was asleep.

Chapter 13

The Silver Lining

"Chelsea, seriously—you need to get *up*. We're leaving in an hour."

My eyes were still closed, but I could hear the distinct voice of my younger sister coming from the doorway of our bathroom.

"For what?"

"Uh, my *graduation*? So get up!."

Fuck! In the midst of my hangover and romantic adventures over the past two days, I had forgotten about her graduation. And it was raining! *At least it would be inside.*

"Is it inside?"

"No. Outside still."

Great, I got to spend the day listening to inspirational speeches made by kids that don't know the first thing about the world, and I was going to do it all while sitting outside, in the rain.

It wasn't until I was fully immersed in my shower that all the thoughts I had about Chris and Drew came flooding into my head. I did the only responsible thing and made a mental pro and con list. Drew won the job category seeing as how he'd secured a position as a financial analyst at a company that valued him enough to let him move cross country and Chris, well I wasn't sure what he was doing but I was fairly certain it wasn't promising. But when it came down to it Chris and I connected on a level that I didn't know if I would ever have with anyone else. But Drew never broke my heart like Chris did and that was something I couldn't ignore, even if I wanted to.

Like most pro and con lists, after completing it, I knew no more than I did before—I still didn't know which was the right choice. Maybe what pro and con lists teach is that you neither choice was preferable, and maybe that was true for me. Maybe I didn't really like the idea of ending up with *either* of them.

It was 12:30 by the time I got out of the shower, and I knew I needed to really speed up the getting ready process, unless I wanted to actually look as depressing as my life suggested. In the female ritual, we insisted getting ready took an hour, when it usually took only thirty minutes, which meant I was only going to get to see three episodes of *Sex and the City* instead of four, but sacrifices needed to be made.

I couldn't change the fact that, in three hours, I would be repeatedly admitting that I had no job, but I could change how I looked. I'd have my good looks going for me, and at least then everyone would be thinking that I'd be married soon, so my future would seem brighter, or at least I hoped.

As I sat on my bed, I saw that blinking red light, taunting me, and I knew what was waiting on the other end. I had to look, to find out which of my two suitors had left me a long, romantic text message, begging me to be with them. Grabbing the phone, I took a deep breath and pressed the unlock button.

1:35 pm Mom: We're leaving in half an hour.

Being a major fan of old black and white movies, I could never decide which was more depressing: waiting by an old, dial telephone in a floor length gown, or opening a text you thought was from a boy and finding out it was from your mother?

Even though I would have a very busy day filled with forced reminiscing on the days when I had some remote success in my life, it still bothered me that neither had reached out to me. So like any normal female on the planet, I spent the next half an hour making a mental note of all the reasons they *hadn't* texted me, with two reasons seeming more plausible than the rest:

1) They had been in tragic accidents involving a runaway tiger from the Philadelphia Zoo and were dead.

2) Sobriety and the morning light had brought them to the conclusion that I was just another "great" girl, but not the one.

They were still sleeping, or maybe they were just waiting for me to text them, didn't seem likely to me. I suddenly felt nauseous, I needed to lie down. I just put my head on the pillow when I heard my mom's voice calling to me.

"Chelsea—time to go. Come downstairs."

One of the worst parts about living at home—you can never purposefully be late to family functions. For some reason, I didn't think my parents were going to buy the excuse, "Sorry, I was stuck in traffic."

Peeling myself from the bed, I made my way downstairs, feeling worse than ever about going back to my high school stomping grounds.

"I can't believe Sarah's graduating today. It feels like, not that long ago, we were watching the two of you walking across the stage—off to start your life!"

My family was never one for sharing emotions, but lately my mom became emotional whenever we hit a major milestone... or when she heard children singing.

"Yeah, and look how far *we* got!"

I had the youth of a 22-year-old and the cynicism of a 53-year-old man.

After pulling into the parking lot, and we walked along the track to our seats on the edge of the football field, I thought about the events that had led up to that moment.

"Any updates on the job hunt?"

"No, nothing." Why did he have to bring this up? I would have said something if I got a job.

"You know the reason why I'm hardest on you, or why you feel I'm hardest on you is because I know when you're being pushed you can accomplish so much."

"Yeah, well apparently not this time. It feels like I can't accomplish anything."

"It'll happen, eventually. Just give it some time."

His hand squeezed my shoulder.

"And in the meantime, I'm supposed to do what? Just sit around and do nothing?"

"No, you keep doing what you're doing. Keep working on your designs. Get your name out there. You keep pushing forward until you get there."

I shrugged my shoulders. I didn't really know what he wanted me to say.

"I love you and your sisters equally. Really, I do. And you've all got your own talents, but one thing that you have that your sisters don't is an ability to really go after what you want. Most kids would have taken any job they could find, but you're really going after a dream. I'm proud of you for that."

My nose started to feel hot as the tears were about to come. I started to wonder if there was ever going to be a time in my life that I wasn't about to cry.

"I don't feel like I'm making anyone proud."

I wiped my eyes with the edge of my hand.

"You and Mom have done so much for me, you've given me everything you could to make sure that I can get what I want out of life. I feel like I'm working hard, that I've been working hard, and I'm just getting nowhere. It's so hard to wake up every , feeling like I've disappointed you."

He stopped walking and placed his hands on my shoulders so I had to face him directly.

"Listen to me," he said in a stern but soft voice. "All I ask is that you work hard and do your absolute best. That's all I've ever asked of any of you."

I sniffled and looked down at my feet.

"You have big dreams, and the only way to get there is through a steep, rough climb. It's not easy, and sometimes you're going to fall, but your mother and I will always be here to support you and pick you back up."

"Yeah, I know."

I felt a few tears fall down my cheek and I quickly wiped them away.

"There's nothing disappointing about having a daughter who has the courage to chase after her dreams. Not a lot of parents can say that about their kids. I'm proud of you for that, really I am."

He pulled me toward him and hugged me for a long time.

"Now, if it doesn't work out the way you want it to, you will have to get *some* sort of job because there will come a time that you will have to move out of the house."

We both laughed and started to walk towards the stadium.

There would still be times when I could tell he couldn't quite put his finger on who I was or why I did things the way I did them, but it felt good knowing he was still proud to have me as his daughter—that I hadn't let him down.

Maybe the point wasn't trying to understand each other, maybe what made a family a family, was not having to figure everyone out but standing by them and loving them in spite of how different you all may feel.

With the evening sun shining on the football field of Hattington High School, pictures of prom, senior week down the shore, Friday night football games and happiness were right before me. I had almost become convinced that maybe life didn't get better after high school, when all the memories that the pictures don't show came back to light.

All of a sudden, I remembered the tears, the self-doubt and the broken hearts that surrounded each and every memory. For the first time in a long time, I didn't think about high school as an easier time. I felt confident that four years into the future, I'd look back on the tough times I was experiencing as an unemployed post grad, and I would remember only the laughs, while forgetting there were ever tears.

Just then I heard a voice behind me. I knew who it was. Smiling, I turned around.

"What are you doing here?"

Drew's sport coat fit perfectly, I hadn't seen him so dressed up in years, so I'd forgotten how good he looked when he put in a little effort.

"What do you mean? You think I'd miss the Hattington High School Graduation? It's the highlight of my social season."

I rolled my eyes and smirked.

"I'm serious! Do you have a younger sibling I don't know about?"

"Fine, fine. Seriously, I'm here with Mike."

He nodded toward the bleachers and I waved to one of our friends.

"Right. I forgot—his brother is in my sister's grade."

"Yeah,"

He paused for a second, looking around.

"About last night..."

"Oh, don't worry about it," I interrupted. "We can just forget the whole thing."

"Oh?" he said surprised. "Yeah, sure. I guess I'll get back to Mike now. I am officially his date."

"That's probably a good idea—he *did* take you to the biggest social event of the season, after all."

"Right," he laughed. "I'll see you around."

His hand brushed against mine as he walked away. Maybe it was just the nostalgia of being back at my old high school—where we'd first become so close, but I felt my heart sink a little as I watched him walk away.

"Actually no, I don't *want* to."

I was about to sit back down when I saw him walking towards me again.

"What are you talking about?"

"I don't want to just forget about the whole thing."

"Drew, you don't have to do this."

My heart was racing as I looked around. My family was talking with the other parents—too far away to hear.

"I know, but I *want* to."

He leaned toward me, his hands on my waist as he kissed me.

"I like you, I really, really like you," he whispered.

Just then, I felt my phone vibrate in my purse. It was Chris.

Chris: 4: 15 pm: I'm having some people over tonight. See you around 8?

"Is that Chris?"

I looked up from my phone at the sound of his voice.

"Oh, yeah. It's nothing." I threw my phone back into my bag.

"Drew! How are you? I haven't seen you in so long. Somehow, I must have missed you at the party the other night."

My mom had found us.

"I'm good, Mrs. Carlton. I should probably get back to my seat, It looks like the speeches are gonna start soon."

"Well, it was great seeing you!"

My mom hugged him before sitting down. He leaned into me and slipped one arm around my waist.

"Think about what I said. I'm not going anywhere—not anymore."

And with that, he walked away. It sent a chill down my spine and it felt like hours before I could move my legs and sit down.

"What was *that* about?" Rachel asked as she nudged my leg with her own.

"What was *what* about?"

"That kiss. Do you think I'm *blind?*"

"Oh, I don't know."

"Tell me."

"It was nothing, seriously."

"Girls, please stop talking. The speeches have started, and we're here to celebrate Sarah, remember?" my dad scolded.

"Tell me later," Rachel whispered.

I just rolled my eyes and tried to focus on the ceremony and not the major decision I had in front of me.

If I went to Chris' house that night, then my future with Drew was probably over. The idea of a relationship with Drew felt right, but I still wasn't sure if I was ready to let go of Chris for good.

Three inspirational speeches later, I sat, watching my younger sister walk across the same stage that started my journey four years earlier. She would inevitably outshine me, since she was going to end up as some top-of-the-line orthopedic surgeon one day. But what else were younger siblings for, if not to one-up the sibling before them?

I pulled out my phone to take a few pictures, and as the graduates of the Class of 2014 stood and threw their caps in the air, an email came through.

Subject: Job Opportunity
Chelsea,
I hope everything's going well for you. One of our junior designers just left, so a position has opened up and it's yours if you want it.
Best,
Lee

I'd been waiting so long to see an email that didn't start with, "Thanks for your interest..." that I wasn't sure what to feel. At last, my life had started to come together.

We spend so much time fighting fate and searching for something more, but once we get out of our heads and accept that, although life may look different than we once thought it would, it doesn't mean the value of it is any less—we can find the strength to move forward.

In the end, life is full of disappointment and heartbreak, with a few precious, fleeting moments of pure happiness, and yet somewhere along the way, the sadness gets pushed to the back, and when we look back on life, all we're left with is memories of how great it all once was.

I texted the first person who came to mind:

5:30 pm: I got a job! I'm moving to New York.

And it was in that moment that I knew he was the one I wanted to be with—the *only* one.

ABOUT THE AUTHOR

Jenni Fink, a part-time writer and full-time real world navigator began her writing career with Buzzfeed as a community contributor and the satirical lifestyle blog, *Frankly Fink.* She considers this author bio one of her greatest literary works— it isn't every day you get to promote yourself in the third person. *Sentenced To Life* is her first novel, she currently lives in New Jersey and is working on her second novel.

Acknowledgements

First, above everyone else, I would like to thank God for making this dream of mine come true. I'm not an extremely religious person but seeing as how you probably won't read much farther than this I wanted to make sure to thank God for all the work He's done in my life, sometimes I don't think we give Him enough credit.

Christopher Moebs, thank you for believing in this work from the very beginning and sharing in my vision of how great of a story it could be when few others did. Also, for recommending my editor, Brandy Alexander. Without her, people would still be reading multiple three page paragraphs and forty page chapters.

Marcus McGee, thank you for continuously putting up with my incessant series of text messages, emails and panicked phone calls about my new ideas. You've been an amazing guide through this entire process, if publishing doesn't work out you'd make an excellent life coach.

Kara Barling, Alex Failla and Tess Givnish, your work on the cover of this book literally brought my vision to life. Also, thank you for letting me pay you primarily in appetizers.

Morgan Hultquist and Rachel Lichtman, your confidence in my writing and dedication to reading early versions kept me going and I'll always be grateful for that. Rachel, without you telling me to select and practically all of the first half of the book, my manuscript would be sitting in a trash bin somewhere instead of on my bookshelf.

Keira DiSpirito, Callie Reid and Maria Lanza. Thank you for still hanging around after over a decade, you've been a source of strength, laughter and above all, my inspiration. With our lives changing, one thing remains constant, your ability to be there for me in the good times and the hard times and for that I'll always be grateful. (Which is good because if this book doesn't work out I'm gonna need to sleep on one of your couches rent-free. Thank you in advance.)

Finally, to my family. It's not every-day I get to publicly thank you for all you've done for me but I'll keep it short since you're probably the only ones still reading anyways (and it's probably because I'm standing over your shoulder making sure you keep reading until the bitter end.) You gave me everything just so I could have a chance at a piece of my dreams. Your unconditional support and drive to push me to be far beyond the best I imagined I could be got me to this point. I owe you more than I could put into words (If you're mentally calculating the money I saved in therapy when you talked me down from various stress-induced mental breakdowns please stop, because you can't put a price on public on a public acknowledgement, right?)

This is because of you. Thank You.

order at www.pegasusbooks.net

CPSIA information can be obtained at www.ICGtesting.com
Printed in the USA
LVOW10s0011150715

446166LV00001B/5/P